The Temple of the Incubus

Ryan Keith Johnson

All songs, poems via compositions are written by the author, Ryan Keith Johnson
Compositions can be found in the book;
"What I Think About You" Song Lyrics and Poetry

Mother Bitch
Driving Nails Down Your Spine
Love Triangle
Mother Bitch II
Idiots Like You
Bleeding Through My Eyes
Souls Under The Floor
Angry At You
I Begin My Aversion From You

ISBN   978-0-615-55578-2

Cover Design by Ryan Keith Johnson

Other books by the author;
The King's Retribution
What I Think About You
Lion Ascend

Shannon woke up and screamed while rising up from her bed. The fifteen year old was in a cold sweat. She endured six months of nightmares and it was tormenting her. The name Incubus filled her brain while bits and pieces of the temple that rummaged such mind. Shannon Anna Lewis didn't believe in the high lord, but she thanked God to be awake. It had been the fifth nightmare this week and they were getting more violent. Shannon had read books on dreams and tried to interpret them, but the information she applied failed. There was the idea to seek out a dream catcher, but when she hung it up above her bed it failed. The teenager asked a good witch to cast magic to protect her and was told to ask Arch Angel Michael for protection, but it failed. She even went to great lengths to get a statue of Mary and a painting of Jesus. It seemed strange, but it gave her room a sense of power. It grew to her attention that after the nightmares the statue of Mary was crying in tears and blood fell upon Jesus' cheeks. Like everything else they failed, the night continued with the onslaught of nightmares and Shannon lost faith. Her mother, Sharon, asked her what the problem was, but when

Shannon told her she received criticism that they were only nightmares. Like everything else in Shannon's life her mother failed.

The teenager checked her clock to see that it was just after four-thirty in the morning. She let out a yawn while lying back in bed to relax. Her dark blue eyes turned to the most recent school picture of her in a soccer jersey with her team mates. She was beautiful with long blonde hair that was quite often high lighted with blonde streaks. Her natural hair color was dark blonde, but unlike most dumb blondes she was smart, but not a straight "A" student. Then she looked at the black and white picture of her mother with the baby, the baby was Shannon. She missed those old times when she wanted to be just like her mom, but now those days were gone and she could only be herself.

Shannon rose out of bed and looked into the mirror to see how she looked. The troubled teen tried to remember the dream that scared the hell out of her. As she crept close to the mirror she saw how pale she was and felt sticky from sweat. It was a gross feeling and she didn't want to endure it any longer. Shannon wiped the sweat off her forehead and thought about the nightmare. The name Incubus once again emerged from her mind.

She took a deep breath and turned around to her dresser. A change of clothes would do as well as a new attitude for a fresh new day. Shannon selected the clothes that suited such needs as well as her sense of fashion. She not only had to please herself, but her classmates as well. After making her choices along with the make up bag there was the trip to the bathroom. Shannon opened her door and looked around to see it was dark in the hallway. She was scared of the dark and since the nightmares persisted to take over her body and soul it became difficult to take the steps.

"Come on Shannon get it together," she said to herself and began walking to the bathroom. Each step of the way she took deep breaths, but heard the Incubus whisper her name in the night. Shannon turned around, but saw nothing and resumed to the bathroom.

Once in the bathroom, Shannon shut and locked the door. With a deep breath she walked over to turn on the water in the shower. It was a simple adjustment to turn the knob to get the right temperature and she removed her clothes as she looked at herself in the mirror. She thought about the love she needed from her mother that was gone a few years ago. The comments of constantly being called a slut from kids at school and her mother devoured her self-esteem until she was now an empty shell. A flashback emerged with the voices of her peers, "you're never going to get a boyfriend because you're not beautiful." Then the sound of her mother's voice entered her mind, "you were out last night with that slut weren't you? What's the matter with you?"

Shannon began to sniffle and cry when she remembered as a child how her mom used to be fun.

Shannon took a deep breath as she wiped her eyes with her hands. It would be easy to sob over this, but it was getting old and she had to overcome this diminished relationship by leaving it behind. Her mother was damaged beyond repair and she had to accept that.

She was hungry, horny and unsatisfied with life. Shannon thought about what was important to her while she brushed her teeth and washed her face to clear her skin. She looked at her tooth brush with Miss Piggy on the handle. Some things from the past you can't forget about, but why was she having these nightmares? Were they warnings of terrible things to come? For all she knew they were warnings of getting pregnant but that didn't make sense because Shannon was still a virgin. She was curious to explore her sexuality, but she was also scared. She didn't want to prove her mother's point of view and didn't want immediately become a whore. When girls her age got laid everyone in school spread rumors about what whores they were. Shannon had got dumped by her boyfriend a couple of weeks ago because he wanted to have sex with her. Shannon didn't want to do it because she wasn't ready, but because he was refused he made her life a nightmare.

The asshole spread terrible rumors that she had crabs and herpes. Many of the girls laughed at her and singled her out during social hours. Maybe that was why she was having these nightmares. Her only desire was to find a guy to fall head over heals for her so she could feel loved. Most girls didn't care about losing their virginity, but for her it was a sacred moment in two people's lives that was shared in intimacy. She dared to dream as she saw steam coming from the shower and turned the CD Player on to a CD by REVERSE and found a song that fit such mood about her ex-boyfriend which was left on repeat, *Driving Nails Down Your Spine;*

if I could get even with you
for all the things that you do
I would be driving nails down your spine
if I could take a knife and stab your heart

The Temple of the Incubus

I would be driving nails down your spine

I do my best to please you
you strike me down
plain as a child
you know I would murder you, for what you do
I hear you laughing at me
treat me like a clown
now I will make others see
of what I mean

you threaten my life
I'll smoke you away
and I'll be driving nails down your spine
you lie to my face
I'll make you a disgrace
I'll be driving nails down your spine
you break my heart
I'll fucken blow you apart
I'll be driving nails down your spine

The water ran hot on her face as steam filled the bathroom and fogged up the mirror. She felt the water run near her mouth while her eyes closed. Shannon's hair was wet with shampoo and she massaged her scalp. She fantasized about making love with a hot guy from school and couldn't wait for it to happen. She imagined him strong and picking her up with his hands on her ass. Even though she never knew what it felt like having a man inside her she had the imagination. It felt good to imagine him sucking as well as biting her neck and massaging her breasts. She opened her eyes and realized it was time to get out. The bathroom was fogging up and she already could imagine her mother banging on the door.

When she got out of the shower the feeling of unrest filled her with fear because the nightmare had fog in it as well. The experience of the Incubus' appearance re-emerged from her nightmares and into her mind as she wiped the mirror with the towel. For a split second she saw a mask and the face was laughing at her. Shannon shrieked and then it was gone. She saw in the mirror how disgusting she looked, her face was pale and her eyes were puffy from crying about the break up. She was not taking care of herself since the break up of Michael, "the asshole". She continued listening to the heavy metal song that was on repeat. Her fingers feathered the foundation and eye shadow around her eyes. She had tricks to hide the undesirable look from her mom, but she would be called a slut and feel empty.

In the past few weeks her mother had become concerned because Shannon appeared to be on drugs. She wasn't on drugs and after more exhausted fights about how Shannon looked or who she hung around with, Shannon's mother withdrew from being tender and understanding. Her mother became cold and would use other people's achievements to put her daughter down. It was Shannon's freshman year and even though she hadn't lost her virginity she wasn't going to give up her curiosity. Her best friend Tammra, a sophomore, explained to her what it was like and what the risk was. Shannon was ready now, ready to pursue her dream and to become a woman.

Shannon walked back into her room with the cordless phone. She was all dressed up, her face full of make up and her hair blow dried. Immediately after the door closed she dialed Tammra's phone number and waited for her to pick up.

"Hello," said a tired voice.

"Tammra?" asked Shannon.

"Shannon?" Tammra groaned.

"What do you want? It's five in the fucken morning. School starts in a few hours and I went to bed at twelve! So this better be good."

"I had that dream again," began Shannon.

"Dream?" asked Tammra.

"Yes, that dream! You know, the one with the evil guy, who wears the mask and is chasing after me in the house. I don't know what to think any more because this has been the fifth time this week that I've had this dream and it's really bothering me," said Shannon.

"Stop watching Friday the Thirteenth and Halloween," replied Tammra.

"I'm not watching TV," declared Shannon.

"You're probably thinking about asshole," said Shannon's best friend, but then there was an uncomfortable silence and Tammra realized she touched an emotional moment. "Ok, I'll tell you what; I'll pick you up in my car and since today is skip day we'll do some catching up."

"Oh, I can't skip today," said Shannon.

"Why not? Today is Friday! We've got to catch up and talk about guys. We've been invited to a party tonight!" exclaimed Tammra.

"I'm sorry, but I've got to pass my English class! Not to mention I'm close to being truant," replied Shannon.

"I'm close to being pregnant," joked Tammra.

"What?" asked Shannon.

"Oh nothing I was making a joke. Listen, life's a bitch if you can't live a little!"

"My life is already fucked up with Michael harassing me at school, my mom calling me names and now the Incubus wants my virginity," replied Shannon as she suddenly heard Tammra laughing.

"I'm serious, I'm having nightmares of this demon chasing after me in tunnels and trying to rape me. I bought a statue of Mary and put her in my room, hoping that she would protect me, but all she does is shed tears. So I bought a painting of Jesus and he starts crying tears of blood. It's like no one gives a shit about me," replied Shannon.

"Well I'll tell you what, I'll be over at your house around seven and we'll go bust the asshole's balls ok! My mom calls me a slut all the time so it's nothing new to me. Your mom is just going through a rough period in her life. As far as the demon in your dream that's all he can do is visit you in your dreams. What you need to do is get a change in attitude and maybe turn on the Christian radio station," suggested Tammra.

Shannon started smiling and giggled, "Yeah right, me and Christian music."

"I'll talk to you at seven," repeated Tammra.

"Ok thanks, see you here," Shannon answered as she hung up the phone.

The teenager was depressed about how things were going and wanted to escape. Shannon thought about running away or committing suicide because she was at a breaking point. Finally she rose out of bed, grabbed her head set and CD's. She walked to the kitchen and turned the coffee maker on. After carefully selecting her band "Slave Dancer" she clicked to a song that suited her interest. The song was called Love Triangle. It fit the description of how her life was, a big dump. First, there was the active guitar strumming and the pounding of drums. Then the masculine vocals of a man describing what it was like to be in a love triangle.

you thought it was getting dark out there
he never wanted you at all
after you turned your back on me

The Temple of the Incubus

all I ever wanted from you was one last kiss
and to tell me you never wanted to see me again

When the day grows darker
I can see you love him more
If I could have just one more wish
I'd wish you would scream out my name
and come back in to my arms again
when the days grow longer
I understand you want him more
oh when the days grow stronger
my heart rips and tears from the core

I know its been hard on you
I know he told you lies
It angers me to see that you prefer the abuse
I sleep at night and I hear you calling my name
I leave the phone ringing because I know it's you
the thought of your betrayal leaves my chest in pain

Shannon nodded her head up and down to the rhythm of the song. The sad part of all this was that she ignored a guy who was interested in her while she was navigating blindly in the love triangle relationship. Shannon was pissed off because not only did she lose the guy who was the asshole, but the guy who was interested in her as well. As she cracked open a couple of eggs and put some bread in the toaster there was a pain in her chest, a broken heart.

Before long it was a quarter to seven and she sat at the table eating breakfast. Shannon took off the head set and turned off the music because she thought she heard something. The teenager was sipping her hot coffee when her mother walked into the kitchen. Shannon's mother Sharon was a tall, forty year old woman with a medium build. Her hair was blonde like Shannon's, but it was shoulder length and permed. She was a good hearted lady with only the right intentions, but her opinions of good intention always crippled Shannon's self-esteem. Right away Shannon felt the tension in her shoulders as well as the restrictive energy in the room unfold. Then her mother began talking and it was like the sound of fingernails on a chalk board.

"You left the coffee pot running yesterday," she said.

"Oh did I?" answered Shannon.

"Yes you did, please don't do it again. I don't want to

have a fire in the house."

"I could have sworn I turned it off before I left yesterday," replied Shannon. "Well you didn't, so don't deny it."

Shannon began sulking and continued to eat and thought about the day. Maybe it wouldn't be a bad idea to skip school and who would care if she got truant or failed English. Nobody really cared about high school or anything else that was meaningful.

Her mom sat across from her and started in, "you know, our next door neighbor's kid who's the same age as you passed her SATS with a 133 score and they're sending her off to Harvard.". Shannon turned her eyes away and ignored what was said.

"Did you know that your cousin Emily made the Dean's list," began her mother as she smiled. "Emily's only a year younger than you. Did you hear? She has the opportunity to get into any college she wants."

"Maybe I don't want to go to college," replied Shannon.

"Nonsense, college is a necessity. You can't stay home for the rest of your life and hang around with your slut friend."

"That slut is Tammra," replied Shannon.

"Well, she's a slut and look at how she has you all dressed up. You look like a skanky raccoon."

Shannon got up as the sound of her chair rubbed up against the manolium and slammed the mug of coffee on the table. Her mother looked up at Shannon all surprised and threatened. The two had fights before, but this was the first time in a long time that Shannon fought back.

"Mind your own fucking business! Maybe I don't want to be like you. All the girls at school dress like this and put make up on the way I do. This is how I fit in."

"Don't you dare talk that way to me in my house!" exclaimed Shannon's mom. "I've been at your school and not all the girls dress like a bunch of sluts. I wouldn't be saying this if I didn't care. All the girls that give in to peer pressure have bad parents that let their girls run around half naked with make up on when they're twelve years old."

"As opposed to pressuring me to give up my friends. Compete with the neighbor next door and my cousin. I'm not smart!" exclaimed Shannon.

"All you have to do is apply yourself. You're not even trying to get ahead!" yelled her mother.

"Don't say that," cried Shannon.

"You don't know what I've been going through," she

sobbed.

"Is it men?" asked her mom.

"My friends mean a lot more to me than you do," said Shannon as she began walking away.

"Well tell me, I'm right here!" yelled Shannon's mother as she got up and followed Shannon.

"Fuck you bitch!" shouted Shannon as she walked out and slammed the door in her mom's face.

The old Pontiac Sun Fire rolled up the black top driveway. Shannon ran out of the house upset and in tears. She slammed the door after getting into the car

"Well what are you waiting for? Let's go!" exclaimed Shannon.

"Shannon, what happened?" asked Tammra, but Shannon didn't answer so Tammra backed out of the driveway and peeled out with the music turned up.

I hurt myself this time
were you there for me again?
this time like you said you'd be
I come on home from living hell
all I hear from you is what you hate
what you can't get
what you don't have
you call a living horror

Mother Bitch
you think your great
but your nothing
but a god damn bitch
Mother Bitch
shut your mouth
because what you need is
is a good damn slap
Mother Bitch

I hurt myself again this time
were you there for me again
this time like you said you'd be
All I hear from you is what you hear
I come on home from living hell
what you can't see what you don't have

The Temple of the Incubus

you call a living whore

They were cruising in style with the music blasting really loud while they drove in the car. It was the band REVERSE with the song Mother Bitch. They were singing it on the way to school and enjoying life like any teenage girl.

Tammra was Shannon's best friend and they had been friends since Shannon was in kindergarten. Tammra was a sophomore with beautiful curly blonde hair who was good at listening to Shannon and giving advice. They had been mistaken as sisters, but Tammra received more attention because she had big breasts. Tammra bragged to other friends that she was going to get into modeling and show off her beautiful body. She found out in most agencies you had to be 5'7" and have the look. She worked hard in the gym everyday to stay healthy and fit. Tammra's trade mark was her pretty face especially when people saw her in the year book. She had a white birth mark the size of a freckle just above her lip line. It was similar to Madonna's mole above her lip, but what Madonna didn't have carried over from what Marilyn Monroe had. Tammra's light blue eyes and sweet thin lips captured the attention of guys in any room she walked in.

Tammra turned down the music and looked at Shannon who looked as though something was on her mind. "What's the matter Shannon? You look like shit!"

"That's because I feel like shit, my life sucks. School sucks, my mom's a bitch, my boyfriend dumped me, I have nightmares everyday, and I know I'll never get laid!" Tammra began to smile, "What were you and your mom fighting about?" she asked. Shannon looked at her best friend and didn't answer.

"Were you fighting over me?" asked Tammra.

"More than you can believe. My mom wants to show me off like a show pony. She keeps bragging to me of all the other girls who are smarter, prettier, gifted and so forth. I'm so sick of it and when she brought you up and the other girls I like to hang out with as a bunch of sluts I got mad. I fucken stuck up for myself and you."

"Your mother is totally psycho and over dramatic. I don't sleep around with a bunch of guys and aren't you still a virgin?" Shannon looked away and preferred not to answer.

"Well, your mom obviously doesn't know you," continued Tammra.

"Stick with me girl and you will go places," answered Tammra as she continued to watch the road and was about to turn the music back up when suddenly Shannon started talking.

"So what's the check list with the guys at school?"

"I don't know, Greg has been having his eye on me at every party I've been at," began Tammra.

"Greg, you mean the guy that only has one thing on his mind?" asked Shannon.

Tammra nodded, "Yep," as she rolled her curly long blond hair over her ear and looked into the rear view mirror to see if there were any cops.

"Why is it you attract the men who want to get into your pants and I don't?" muttered Shannon.

"Maybe because I don't look like shit," laughed Tammra as she watched Shannon give her a dirty look

"I was just joking. Look, even though I've done it and I know what it's all about, I'm going to wait until I get married. The guys at school know that I've done it and that is why Greg has his eye on me."

"Yeah, whatever," replied Shannon.

"It's true, it's not that hard to get laid. All you have to do is your homework on the men who are interested and those that aren't. Once you do it a few times it's like eating a Banana Split," smiled Tammra as she licked her lips.

"Please tell me you're joking about the Banana Split part," said Shannon with a confused and discouraged look on her face.

"You really do need to get laid and learn to relax," replied Tammra.

They continued to drive and both girls were quiet. Intuitively Tammra realized Shannon might be angry with her. Her best friend was able to hide behind the façade of make up and eye shadow from other people, but it wasn't enough to fool her. Shannon couldn't fool Tammra and she could feel the weight of stress on her best friend's shoulders. Finally, Tammra pulled over to the side of the road and put the car in park.

"What's wrong?"

"I'm scared Tammra," began Shannon as she turned around to face her best friend.

"Scared of what?" asked Tammra.

"The Incubus," answered Shannon.

"What's the Incubus?"

"I don't know, a demon that rapes me in my dreams. In my dreams, he knows who I am and the little experiences I have and sends his followers after me to bring me to him."

The Temple of the Incubus

"What does he plan to do with you?"

Shannon looked at Tammra and was hesitant to talk about it. She felt awkward sharing such personal information, but she had to tell someone. Tammra was the only one that would lend a friendly ear. They had shared so many adventures together, Shannon felt safe telling her the truth.

"Shannon, tell me what's going on in your dream," demanded Tammra as she watched Shannon lick her lips and prepare to speak.

Shannon looked around the strange room she was in. The room was black and she was lying on a bed that was black with blankets to match. The walls were painted with a strange resin that looked like there were bones and bodies stuck in the walls. Shannon began to shriek at the sight of it and got up from the bed.

There was a strange eerie feeling that she felt was invading her space. The corner of her eye caught movement in the wall. There were faces looking at her, but when she turned around to see what it was, it was only a figment of her imagination. Shannon felt the hair on the back of her neck stand up. The teenager walked over to the door and opened it to see what was there.

Shannon found herself in a long hallway with doors and behind each door she heard noises. The noises were the sound of men and women having sex. The sound of breathing polluted her ears as well as the high pitches of women having orgasms. It seemed very strange to encounter such an episode. Every step of the way the paces of screaming and yelling persisted. Shannon felt embarrassed because she didn't belong there and wondered what she would say if the occupants caught her.

All the doors were closed except one and she became interested in what was behind the door. There was screaming, shouting and a woman having an orgasm. Shannon carefully slid open the door and walked in to see what was going on. She could see a short hallway with white paint and what looked like sunlight coming

12

in from windows that were draped. Even though they were draped they allowed a crack of light to come through. Shannon could see there was a small kitchen and finally came across the living area. She saw a white bed with white blankets and bed spread. By the way the blanket moved she knew that there were two people having sex, but then the blanket moved aside revealing the two people. Shannon was shocked to see herself naked and all sweaty with a man with long black hair on top of her. She saw the man turn his head to face her and she realized that he was the Incubus. It looked like he was wearing a mask that was attached to his face. He revealed an `evil smile with sharp teeth,

> *"Shannon you belong to me!" he* growled.

Tammra stared at her best friend after hearing about the dream. Shannon looked scared and turned to stare out the window. The two friends were quiet until Tammra broke the ice, "wow I don't know what to say?"

Shannon looked away from her best friend. Tammra could tell by the expression on Shannon's face that she was ashamed for talking about the dream. Tammra could now see why her best friend was hesitant about having sex. The Incubus was inside Shannon's head and giving her nightmares of a good thing. Then Tammra took a deep breath and began thinking about her own experiences. For something so little to lose there was so much to gain for greater experiences with better men in the future. It seemed over dramatic for Shannon to act this way. Tammra couldn't understand why it was so important for her best friend to keep her virginity even with the nightmares. After all, the other girls that lost theirs were happy and moved on to new and better experiences with men. They weren't sitting around fantasizing about it and wishing they had that perfect moment.

"I don't expect you to understand," replied Shannon.

"Shannon, everything will be fine."

Tammra continued driving as Shannon explained the dreams she had. All of a sudden they came across an old mysterious house on the left side of the street. Shannon quickly looked at the house and opened her mouth with a gasp, "pull over for a minute I had a daja vu and feel that I've been to this house before!"

"You've been to this house? Do you want to check it out?" asked Tammra.

Shannon was hesitant, but looked at her best friend, "yes!"

Tammra pulled her car over to the side of the road and both girls got out. The house was a medium size and looked like there hadn't been anyone living in it for years. They got out of the car; walked up to the brown house with old boards and two windows in the front with a window on the door. It had a small porch in the front with an old table and chair.

Shannon walked around by the windows and peeked inside to see the furniture was covered with white linen. There was an eerie chilling feeling that touched her. She turned to her best friend and she was being creeped out.

"The house appears to be empty and abandoned," said Shannon.

"Great," began Tammra, "can we leave now?"

Shannon tried to open the door, but it was locked. "Tammra do you remember this house ever being here in the first place?" asked Shannon. Tammra shook her head, "I've been to busy to keep track of the houses."

"I don't remember this house being here. I remember an empty lot," replied Shannon.

Shannon and Tammra looked at each other for a minute and the wind died down. Neither one knew what to say about exploring the house. Shannon wanted some excitement in her life and skip school.

"What do you want to do?" asked Tammra as she pulled out a brush and began combing her hair back.

"I don't know, something is calling me inside and I don't know what it is," said Shannon.

"Well you better decide because I don't want to be here and I don't want to be at school," replied Tammra as she looked at her watch.

"That's interesting, you don't want to be here or at school. Where would you like to be then?"

"Shopping at the mall, to find some sexy clothes to wear," said Tammra as she noticed there was a pause from Shannon who knew her friend a little better than that.

"Oh come on Shannon, what do you want? You want to go exploring some dead beat up house that probably has some old lady in there who is about ninety years old and hands out chocolate chip cookies to the dearest of her heart. No, I don't think so! This building is condemned and about to fall apart. I just bought my two-hundred dollar pair of blue jeans yesterday and I'm not going to get them dirty. I'm also not getting cob webs in my hair."

"Listen I tell you what, I had a dream and this house was in it. I just want to explore it up close. We're not going to roll around on the floor and we're not going to get into trouble," assured Shannon.

"Fine," replied Tammra.

Shannon walked up to the door followed by Tammra. She pulled out a paper clip and unbent it to stick in the key hole. Tammra began sulking and sighed just as she turned around. There was a huge commotion of screaming and Shannon turned around to see what was going on.

Two high school boys named Eddie and Greg were right behind them. Greg was a big boned senior with blonde hair and stood about six inches taller than Tammra. He was wearing a tanktop with his jacket wrapped around his waist and showed off his muscular arms. The teenager was very handsome and was every girl's sex symbol in high school. Rumors spread through out the high school of how he performed in bed. Greg was a jock and besides playing hockey, football and track he only had one thing on his mind. Girls never seemed to get it through their heads that he was using them for sex. Eddie, the drug addict, was a junior with a skinny bone frame, brown hair and green eyes. He was a complete burn out and did every kind of drug imaginable, but his favorite was smoking pot because it slowed his mind down.

Eddie always had a sour look about him as if he was always stoned. He was usually hanging out with Greg, snorting cocaine and banging some bimbo that Greg picked up from off the street. Greg had rich parents and used that to his advantage to pick up chicks.

"Scared you didn't we!" laughed Greg as he watched Tammra close her eyes and let out a sigh.

"If you guys ever try that shit again I swear to God I will dump a ton of sugar down each of your gas tanks," exclaimed Tammra.

"I would settle for cocaine and a night with you sweet heart," replied Eddie as he smiled. "Yeah whatever, in your dreams," replied Tammra.

"I'd get you all puckered up with cocaine and I'd watch you jump on top of me like a bunny," he laughed.

"You really do need to shut up," insisted Tammra.

"What he meant is he would like to spend a night with a girl who looks similar to your standards," corrected Greg as he smiled. Tammra didn't say anything and turned around to look at Shannon who rolled her eyes and looked just as puzzled.

"Shut up," said Shannon. Greg whispered to Eddie and then saw Tammra turn around to face him. "Ok we're sorry about coming out of the corner of the house like that. It was wrong and we won't do it again," apologized Greg.

"Good God, you guys scared the shit out of me," repeated Tammra.

"What's up?" asked Greg as he looked around. Both girls looked at him and wondered if they could use him to get in the house. Tammra turned to Shannon, smiled and right away they both had a plan in place.

"What are you guys doing at this old house anyway?" asked Eddie.

"Because we can," answered Shannon as she looked at Eddie and Greg.

"Greg, do you remember this house ever being here?" asked Shannon. Greg was silent as he tried to think for himself, "I don't know. It's just a house, I for one have been too busy to know."

"That's the weird thing, I've lived in this town for a long time and I for the life of me do not remember this house ever being constructed. It's like it was built here over night," replied Shannon.

"So is that what you're doing? Exploring and investigating it?" asked Eddie.

"We're making a commitment to see who lives here," insisted Tammra.

"You could say I'm looking for answers," said Shannon.

"An excuse to skip school, Shannon?" asked Greg as he folded his arms and smiled. "No it has nothing to do with that," she answered.

"Can we come with you since we aren't going to school either?" asked Eddie. Shannon and Tammra looked at each other with light smirks on their faces. It would be nice to have a couple of men watching out for them if they were in trouble.

"Sure," answered Shannon.

Tammra nodded as well, but it was not the house that scared her it was the feeling of being watched or raped. The nightmare Shannon told her scared her because a beautiful girl was always a target by lesser men.

The Temple of the Incubus

As Greg walked towards the entrance he saw there was a big window in the door and broke the glass with his fist. Tammra immediately felt an attraction towards him and looked at his strong muscular arms. The jock turned his head and smiled at her as he reached through the broken window of the door and unlocked it.

"Don't get the wrong idea that I break into houses," smiled Greg,

"I don't have any assumptions about you. I'm only here for my best friend," assured Tammra as she winked at him. Greg opened the door while thinking about how much of a slut Tammra was and turned his head to both girls, "ladies first."

Shannon and Tammra looked at each other and walked in the house. Greg was looking at both girls' body parts and was licking his lips as he looked at Tammra's ass.

"What do you think?" asked Eddie.

"They'll be good housewives someday," began Greg as he unraveled his coat around his waist and put it on.

"Not the girls you idiot, the house," said Eddie, but he could already tell Greg was interested in Tammra.

The four teenagers walked into the porch. There was another door that was unlocked so they walked through to see what was inside. They saw it was gloomy and as they walked further, they found themselves in the living room with a wooden floor. Shannon could see the furniture was covered with white linen to keep the dust off, but why? It's not like anyone would buy the house unless they were a family of axe murderers.

The light coming through the window curtains left shadows on the walls. Tammra looked at a small table against the staircase and saw a strange looking chest. As she walked towards it, she could see it was black with gold trimming on the edges. In the center, where the key hole was, there was a depiction of what looked like a mask with its eyes protruding down with an evil sneer. Tammra had the temptation to open it, but then turned her head to see if anyone was looking.

"This place gives me a chilling feeling and I don't like it," complained Shannon as she looked around. "Then why did you want to come in?" asked Greg.

"I wonder who lived here?" asked Greg as he began to walk up the stairs.

"Somebody who had a sick sense of humor," replied Tammra.

"I think this place would make a good hide out," said

Eddie.

"What do we have here?" asked Greg as he walked over to the chest that Tammra was looking at.

"Somebody left this here," said Tammra as she watched Shannon and Eddie walk over to see it.

"Why would somebody leave this here?" asked Greg.

Shannon suddenly freaked out when she saw the front of the chest was an open lock with the evil looking mask, "oh my God, oh my God its him!"

"Who?" asked Eddie and Greg.

"That's what he looks like?" asked Tammra. Shannon nodded her head and looked hysterical, "yes."

"Well you know, since you found the chest you have to open it," began Greg.

"I'm not opening that chest," answered Tammra.

"Aren't you a little bit curious?" asked Eddie.

"Not in the least," replied Tammra.

"It could be some expensive jewelry from a treasure hunt," began Greg, "besides it's only a stupid chest." Suddenly Tammra had a change in attitude and became curious.

"You can keep whatever is inside," said Greg. Tammra put her hands over the top of the chest and unfastened the lock that wasn't clamped together to open it. Suddenly there was a huge gust of wind that emanated from the chest and sucked the teenagers inside.

The four teenagers woke up and found themselves on the wooden floor of the house. Tammra and Shannon rose up and looked around just as the guys did and saw that they were in the same spot that the chest left them. Tammra looked to see the chest that she opened was gone, but they didn't know what happened and assumed that nothing happened.

"What happened?" asked Eddie.

Shannon looked around and became scared as she noticed the walls were the same black oily look that was in her dream. She could see things moving in the walls like a nightmare animation of hands and legs. What scared Shannon the most was the red eyes that stared at her from the walls. They stared at her with a steady glow and once she blinked they were gone.

"Oh my God! This can't be happening!" she began crying as a picture emerged in her mind of a past nightmare. One of her nightmares was her walking down the aile to get married to the Incubus. It was known to her in the dream as a Virgin Marriage and the way the Incubus would empower himself over Shannon.

Tammra walked up to comfort her, "what's the matter?" she whispered as Shannon's eyes opened up. Shannon covered her mouth and closed her eyes as tears streamed down such trembling cheeks. "We're inside my dream," Shannon squeaked while she was crying. Suddenly Tammra felt goose bumps on her arms and the hair on the back of her neck stood up.

Greg and Eddie looked at each other confused after looking around and seeing the nightmarish arms and hands coming out of the walls.

"I feel like I'm in some fucked up acid trip!" said Eddie. Greg looked around and saw the staircase leading up connecting to two other staircases going up to either side. "This is not the same house we entered," said Greg.

After about fifteen minutes Shannon calmed down and was able to function on her own and walked over to the guys. She looked at the staircase and saw how diabolical it was in its endless maze with other staircases going upwards. As strange as it was there was light all over the house and the sensible thing to do was escape.

"Does anybody want to leave?" asked Shannon. Greg nodded his head, "I've seen enough."

"I'll second that," agreed Tammra.

They walked back to find the entrance where they had broken into should have been only twenty feet away. Shannon's heart beat faster and faster as she prepared for the worst. Tammra's mouth dropped as she saw nothing, but a brick wall.

"Are you kidding me!"

Greg touched it and felt the hard texture. There was no denying it, they were trapped inside the house. Greg turned around to face the girls and looked very disturbed. "What the hell?" said the jock.

"This is fucken bullshit," replied Eddie.

The teenagers walked back to the staircase leading upwards to the crazy crossword puzzle of staircases. Suddenly Shannon freaked out and began crying when she saw someone she didn't want to see. It was the Incubus and three of his associates. Right away the two girls unleashed a terrifying scream and hid behind the guys. Greg and Eddie were scared, but tried to remain calm as they saw the horror before them. They were queer and the leader was in the middle with his arms crossed. They assumed it was a he, but in reality there was no way to know if the leader was male or female. His bone frame was small and his arms were similar to Iggy Pop with long black hair that stretched to the middle of his back. He was dressed in black silky clothes with gold as well as silver bracelets and necklaces with a mask to hide his face. His followers were dressed the same way and looked very odd. The two females had no tops and only wore black thongs. The other associate was big and muscular with no shirt, but a pair of black silky pants.

The mask of the Incubus was white and animated to his facial expression. It wasn't able to be taken off and the teenagers could see a vile smile emerge on it. His eyes were black and looked hollow as though there was nothing inside his head.

The host began to laugh in his deep voice and clapped his hands, "welcome to my home children, I'm your host, the Incubus. These are my associates Ezela, Shanga and Tic Tock." Ezela and Shanga looked like they were female because of their long black hair, Tick Tock looked male and had very little hair on his head. The three of them were nearly naked and their bodies were inside out. If you've ever seen a body inside out you can imagine seeing blood, veins and all the organs. They had no eyes only eye sockets and skin with blood over their face. Tammra leaned down and puked on the floor when she saw the way their bodies were contorted. The strange part was that his associate's bodies were also black and oily.

"What do you want?" asked Greg stuttering in fear.

"I want you. I want your girls to be a part of my temple," replied the Incubus.

"You sick son of a bitch, are you planning to kill us?" asked Greg.

"No, it's more like warp your mind, kill you, destroy your soul and then turn your body inside out so you become my decibel or shadow," answered the Incubus.

"Well I'm not going down without a fight," said Greg as he raised his fists in the air.

"Tick Tock take care of my light work," ordered the Incubus. Tick Tock began walking towards Greg with a long bone in his hand while the other was in a fist and had a fat grin on his zombie like face. Greg looked at the decibel and was scared when he saw what he would look like.

"Stupid teenager, you should never have entered the house," said Tick Tock with a deep growl. He raised the long bone that looked like it was part of a human leg and busted it with both hands. Greg gasped and felt pain in his diaphragm as though someone was stabbing him with knives. The girls began crying and didn't know what to think because they were trapped.

"You see this is what's going to happen to you. I bust you to pieces like I did to this bone. You're just a stupid, dumb, teenage, popular kid in your world. In this world you're a low life," growled Tick Tock. Just when the creature threw the bones to the floor he raised his fist to strike Greg. Suddenly, Shannon stepped out from behind Greg and stood in front of Tick Tock and cried, "please don't hurt him." Tick Tock stopped and watched her run up to the Incubus, "please be merciful and let us live!"

"Shannon, what are you doing?" whispered Tammra.

Ezela and Shanga stood in the way to keep Shannon in line. The Incubus looked at Shannon and revealed an evil smile. He walked closer and gestured his Shadows to step aside. The Incubus looked at the fifteen year old girl with admiration as well as courage.

"You're so pure and childlike. What is your name, girl?" asked the Incubus.

"Don't you know who I am? You've been in my dreams," said Shannon with fear in her voice.

"I've been in all dreams, especially those who value virginity. I don't keep track of names," said the Incubus.

"My name is Shannon and these are my friends Tammra, Eddie and Greg. Please don't hurt us, we didn't mean to trespass in your domain. I beg you, please let us go?" she began crying and felt the pain of pins pierce her skin.

"I don't let anybody go," began the Incubus. "I need to feed off you to keep my strength."

"Please, this isn't fair. Give us a chance to escape," begged Shannon as she continued crying.

The Incubus nodded and gestured Tick Tock to leave Greg alone and return. "I tell you what. I'll give you thirteen hours to escape and every clock is accurate. Once the clock strikes thirteen o' clock you belong to me," declared the Incubus as he and his followers disappeared from sight.

Shannon looked at her best friend and upper classmen from school. Everyone was scared and didn't know what to do. Shannon took a deep breath as she put her left hand over her mouth and thought about the nightmares. She put her foot on the first step while thinking about Michael the asshole that made her life a living hell. The teenager removed her hand from her mouth to grip the railing as she felt pain in her chest. Shannon was the first, followed by the other three, to walk up the stair case. The stairs were old and creaky, but they soon began to magically change into brand new hard floors. Along the walls, which were also changing from old to new, they saw paintings of the Incubus with many associates and they were all sneering. The teenagers also saw paintings of the Incubus having sex with teenage girls. The girls in the paintings looked like they were in a lot of pain, but the Incubus was enjoying himself. There were paintings of animals, big and small with their bodies turned inside out. There were even paintings of the women that were inside out, seducing teenage boys. The teenagers moved along from the creepy paintings to the top of the staircase. The dirty lights and chandeliers hanging in the ceiling suddenly became clean.

"I don't believe this," said Tammra.

"What?" asked Greg.

"The chandelier in the ceiling was really dirty and now it's clean."

"This whole place is changing," said Shannon.

It took twenty minutes to get to the top, but once they made it they took a minute to rest. Eddie looked down to see how far the stairs went and couldn't believe how far they had walked. The length of the stairs seemed to have grown since they started the journey. They looked to either side to find there was nothing but the floor and two sets of staircases that went about ten feet to the top. Shannon picked the one on the right and continued to the next floor.

"The second floor, I presume," whispered Shannon. Tammra, Greg and Eddie were right behind her and were curious about the rest of the house. They were as amazed as she was and could not imagine how scary this house could really be. The four teenagers reached the top of the staircase and looked around. They turned around to see on the bottom where the Incubus and his associates used to be.

"Oh, I think I'm going to get sick," began Tammra.

"That would be one hell of a drop," began Eddie. Shannon looked both ways of the long path and decided to go to the left. As they walked, Shannon could see the awkward wall that surrounded the entrance of the corridor and it was in the shape of an ass.

"Shannon are you sure you want to go in there?" asked Greg.

"We're walking in someone's ass," laughed Eddie, but he realized he wasn't getting any attention because everybody seemed more interested in looking for an escape.

They spent the better half of the thirteen hours exploring the hallway filled with rooms. They explored the rest of the temple and realized it was huge. There were no exits outside and it frightened the girls because they were afraid of getting raped. Shannon could feel the penetration of a man's organ push into her insides with strong thrusts. She had no experience, but heard from girls that they were sore and bleeding. No girl would ever think about walking home alone at night because there was a chance of getting raped, but these were different circumstances. Greg and Eddie wouldn't be able to prevent them from getting raped by the decibels. They did however find startling clues from engraved pictures on the walls of the rooms and hallways. There were images of mirrors, creatures fighting humans, the Incubus sitting on a throne and being worshiped by his followers. There were depictions of a girl restrained in a position that showed the Incubus having sexual intercourse with her.

The temple was huge and had more rooms, corridors, and thrones than could be imagined. The rooms they entered were nothing more than the chambers of a teenager's bedroom. They looked pretty ordinary; bed, dresser, toys and knick knacks. Shannon realized there was something odd, every room didn't have a mirror. Usually every teenager would have a mirror hanging on the wall, especially a girl. Each room had a stale and bland feeling in them as though they were empty.

The teenagers could feel the temple changing shape wherever they walked and manipulated its passage as they proceeded. The walls were filled with pictures similar to Egyptian hieroglyphics and old swords. Shannon walked over to the swords and looked at them. Her friends were busy looking at statues, dolls, paintings and other art work. Shannon took one of the daggers off the wall and looked at it. She placed the blade on the palm of her hand and dug into it. For a minute the pain was severe, but after Shannon cut herself she watched the blood fill her hand. Then, before her eyes, the blood renounced back into the wound and healed. Shannon's mouth dropped and began whimpering after thinking this was all a dream. A dream that wouldn't allow you to wake up in your bed, safe and sound.

As the hours persisted, the teenagers realized that they had seven hours left before their time was up. Eddie lit up a cigarette after complaining of having nicotine fits. Greg was busy trying to seduce Tammra and staring at her body. Shannon could see there was a huge strain on them so they decided to take a break.

"How are we going to escape from this psycho?" asked Tammra.

"I don't know," replied Shannon.

"You don't know! Well, you better figure it out because I don't want to get raped and killed in this house!" shouted Tammra.

"Girls settle down, I'm sure there is a way out!" assured Greg.

"How? There are no doors, no fucking windows, how do you expect us to get out of here?" yelled Tammra.

"She's right," replied Eddie.

The three of them began arguing as Shannon thought about their predicament. She remembered the hieroglyphics as well as all the queer pictures on the walls and began to realize that the mirrors symbolized the escape from the temple. The way out was through a master mirror, but the only problem was finding that particular mirror. Shannon felt a daja vu come over her and just knew certain events were happening about five minutes before they actually happened. It was exciting at first, but then she realized it was scary and didn't prove to help their escape. Tammra was crying and the guys were cussing about not knowing what to do next.

"Guys!" yelled Shannon as she pulled out the knife she had dropped on the floor and showed her school mates what happened earlier. They watched hysterically as the bleeding hand suddenly renounced and healed.

"This is all a fucking dream and the way out is through a mirror!" exclaimed Shannon.

"A mirror?" asked Greg. Tammra was hysterical and crying.

"What time is it?" asked Shannon. Greg looked at his watch. "Two o'clock, it looks like we won't be going to school," he laughed.

"Oh, so you think this is funny? We're trapped in a fucking maze on a brink of death and all you can think about is school and how funny it is that were going to miss it. I would give anything to be in school!" exclaimed Tammra as she looked at Shannon who was looking at the Incubus' clock.

"Ok, we have about six more hours before the Incubus hunts us down and kills us! Guys I think I have an explanation. We don't have to worry about school because we're not really here," began Shannon not knowing the facts.

"Where are we then?" asked Greg.

"I don't know, probably in our beds or lying on the floor of this old house. One thing is certain we need to escape," said Shannon.

"Do you think we're in another dimension?" asked Greg.

"I don't know, but the Incubus played us from the start," continued Shannon.

"What does he want?" asked Greg.

"Who is he?" asked Tammra.

"What is he?" asked Eddie.

"I'm not sure? I believe he's after me. From what the picture grams say he was created from another world to invade dreams, destroy souls, turn bodies inside out and make us his servants," answered Shannon.

"How do we kill him?" asked Greg.

"I don't think we can," answered Shannon.

"What do you mean we can't?" demanded Tammra.

"I don't know, maybe if we separate to find clues we can escape. I may be able to remember how to escape," said Shannon.

"Why does he want you?" asked Tammra.

"I think he wants me because I'm a virgin," answered Shannon.

"You're still a virgin?" asked Eddie.

"Wow," whispered Greg as he smiled.

"Ok, well big deal," began Tammra, "what has this got to do with anything?"

Shannon turned around away from everybody, "it means I give him power because my soul is pure and my body hasn't been touched."

"Well that is just peachy," began Greg. "What happens to the rest of us?"

Shannon hesitated, "I don't know what he plans to do with you." Then she looked at her friends and realized how weak they were. Tammra began crying and wiped her eyes with the collar of her shirt. Shannon knew that they didn't want to hear it, but she had to tell them.

"Death," she whispered.

"How can we kill something that doesn't die?" asked Eddie.

"You don't," answered Tammra as she stopped crying and got herself together.

"We'll split apart for an hour to find clues of how to escape. We'll come back here and share what we know?" Shannon replied.

"If this is a dream why don't we just pinch ourselves?" asked Greg.

"Why didn't I wake up when I cut my hand with the knife?" asked Shannon.

"We're stuck here."

The teenagers separated and vowed to return in about an hour. Shannon and Tammra decided to explore the second floor in greater detail. Greg and Eddie walked up the stairs to the third floor and hoped they would be successful in finding clues.

"Now, remember, we come back in an hour," yelled Shannon to Greg and Eddie who were on their way upstairs. Shannon looked at her best friend who was exploring the other side of the hallway. Tammra was looking at Shannon and nodded her head before turning around to continue the exploration. The nod was a gesture from Tammra that she would be ok.

Shannon suddenly had a scary feeling that she was being watched and for a second she saw red eyes in the walls, but they vanished. The teenager knew that since it was an endless nightmare that the Incubus would make sure their stay would be hell. Shannon felt he had special plans for them and it wasn't going to be nice. In reality, there was no time in dreams and the Incubus knew he could intervene at any time to scare them. Shannon began walking into the empty rooms that were already explored to see if there were any clues overlooked.

The guys split up and when they got to the top of the third floor Greg went to the right. It wasn't a big deal, but Greg insisted because he saw that Tammra would be just below him. He had the desire to seduce her if she found her way to the third floor with him.

Eddie walked down the hallway of the temple and inhaled his cigarette. He enjoyed the feeling he was getting when the smoke entered his lungs and the chemicals gave him a light headed feeling. He was not paying attention where he was going and didn't care. He suddenly found himself in a chamber full of familiar green plants and he smiled while looking around. There were marijuana plants everywhere that had grown from the floor, the ceiling and the ledges that were attached to the walls. Eddie's mouth dropped as he walked around with the cigarette in his hand. He accidentally dropped it on the ground. "Oh shit," he complained as he stomped on it hoping that it wouldn't start a fire. Eddie clasped his hands together and began laughing.

"Oh God, this is amazing! I've never seen so much pot in

my life!" exclaimed Eddie because it was his dream come true and all he could think about was how much money he was going to make.

"Do you like it?" asked a feminine voice. Eddie screamed after turning his head to see the shadow and tripped onto the floor from his own shoe laces.

"Don't be frightened," it replied. Eddie looked at it and could tell it was a female. She was dark, thin and bony with a face that looked like a mask. The teenager looked at the strange creature and saw its black muscles contorted with bones and organs around its black figure.

"My name is Ezela and I'm the Incubus' shadow," said Ezela as she reached her hand out to Eddie slowly and pulled him up from the ground. The druggy could see she was inside out and twisted. Her hair was long and black.

"What do you want?" he asked. The shadow smiled, "don't you know what I want?" she asked with the stoners smile while holding in front of her a rolled up piece of paper with pot.

"Let's smoke a joint," she whispered and watched Eddie crack a grin while nodding his head.

Greg was walking around the hallway and found more rooms that were unearthly, but all he could think about was having sex with Tammra. He could see more gross pictures of the Incubus and the creatures that were inside out. They seemed to be family pictures that also included the family dog and cat. They were also inside out and looked like they were skinned alive. Greg walked into a room that was large and had shelves of books. He couldn't find anything that sparked his interest until he saw a mirror with a black surface. Greg walked over and could see it was a big mirror that rested on a metallic stand. The teenager looked into it and smiled while taking off his jacket to reveal his tanktop to flex his muscles. Suddenly, he saw something startling and became so scared that he got goose bumps. It was all twenty of his old sex partners in high school and at first they looked at him with innocence then they looked upset. The teenage girls were dressed as he last saw them in his school. Greg began to scream when he saw them stare into his eyes at him as though they wanted to kill him. Then they began coming out of the mirror, looking as real as he was.

"What the fuck is this?" asked the startled teenager.

"Greg, I thought you loved me?" said one of the girls, a pretty burnet.

"I do Nycole, it's just that I wanted some space."

"How much space did you want before you took away my virginity?" asked another girl. Greg turned his attention to the beautiful blonde and his heart sank to see her eyes in tears.

"I thought you loved me and I told my mother you were the one, the one I would marry," she cried.

"Marriage is such a strong word, Krista. I wanted to test our love by testing our love with different people," answered Greg as he realized that they looked like they were going to stampede him.

"You're such a pig," said another one.

"You're such a liar."

"I hope your heart gets so broken that you kill yourself," said another one. They all began to speak united as they called him terrible names and Greg felt a weight of guilt. He put his hands on his ears as he turned around, "shut up!" he yelled.

He turned around and saw that they were gone, but he had tingling sensation on his neck and felt the dryness in his throat. He took a deep breath and had enough of the library and the creepy ex-lovers. He heard strange female whispers; "Greg I want to fuck you over," then when he turned around they ceased. The teenager backed up to the door and there was nothing but the book shelves and the black mirror. Then the next he knew he backed into Tammra.

"Can we get out of here?" she exclaimed.

"No shit!" replied Greg.

The two walked together through the hallway back the way he came until they found a familiar area. Greg turned his head to look at Tammra and immediately fantasized of having sex with her. Tammra turned her head and looked at him.

"What?" she asked.

"Nothing, I was curious as to how you got up to this level?"

"There's another staircase on the second floor and I followed it until I heard you shouting," replied Tammra.

"Oh that, well I was preparing for a yelling match. It helps get my adrenaline rush," smiled Greg as he winked at her. Tammra smiled and continued to walk, "yea ok."

"Oh shit, I got to tie my shoe," he announced as she continued to walk.

Greg pretended to stop and tie his shoe while he was staring at her ass. He imagined with such delight of pounding her with every thrust of his might. Tammra stopped and turned her head, "cut it out and stop staring at my ass!"

The Temple of the Incubus

Greg started laughing and got up from the floor to join her, "I don't know what you're talking about."

Meanwhile, Eddie was having a conversation with Ezela and exchanged a joint. He stood, leaning up against the wall of pot leave and looked at the black arms and hands coming out of the walls. The drug addict couldn't remember another time in his life where he experienced such strange events.

"Does it make you feel good?" asked Ezela. Eddie was stoned and had not felt this high in a long time.

"Yeah, it feels good," he smiled. "So what is this place and what do you do?"

"It's the temple, it's our home," replied the shadow who was smiling.

"So is this basically all you here?" asked Eddie. The Shadow laughed and nodded, "the Incubus seduces teenagers and destroys their souls so their body can be turned inside out," began the shadow. "Virgin girls become his bride until he's taken the entire girl's purity and turns her inside out."

"Wow, that really blows for Shannon because she's a virgin," laughed Eddie. The shadow continued to smile, "Yeah, you won't have anything to worry about. We won't crush your soul and turn your body inside out." Eddie looked into her dark eyes and nodded as she licked her lips and said nothing more.

Tammra and Greg were laughing about old times in school and every thing seemed so right. "The first time I saw you at the party I was thinking who is this hot babe?" began Greg as he heard Tammra continue to laugh. "I had to ask like twenty girls before I could get a name," laughed Greg. "Even then I couldn't get a name. I had to tell them I want to know who the blonde girl's name was." Tammra burst with laughter as she began turning red.

"Well with all the rumors I heard around school about you and the other girls I wasn't sure what to believe," said Tammra as she felt Greg touch her hand.

"Don't believe all the rumors you hear because that's all they are is rumors," said Greg as he moved his head close to Tammra's and kissed her.

Shannon had gotten nowhere with her plan. It seemed like a good plan to begin with, but it was a dead end. She returned to the area where they were suppose to meet and found that nobody was there, "where the hell are they?"

The Temple of the Incubus

Shannon found something very peculiar on the wall of the temple. The walls had pictures engraved in stone of ancient Egypt. Shannon could read the pictures easily and it confirmed such feelings. Mirrors were the key to escape from the temple and were somewhere on the top floor. All of a sudden something quickly emerged out of the brown dingy wall. It was the face of the Incubus.

"You will never escape!" his voice bellowed throughout the hallway.

Shannon jumped back, then fell on the floor and began screaming her head off as she heard the Incubus snarl with a loud screech. Then the face disappeared along with the strange picture graphs back into the wall and laughed at her hysterically.

She quickly got up, turned her head and looked around after seeing the lights from the ceiling flicker off and on in a twelve second interval. She then saw something that was described in the writings as the lazarus. They were animals that were turned inside out and they were running towards her squealing as loud as a train. Shannon did the only thing she could think of, which was run. They were gaining on her each step of the way. Shannon ran through the hallway as fast as she could until her eyes faced a dead end. The teenager turned around in fear and saw the lazarus running straight at her. From the corner of her eye she saw a spot in the wall begin to move back where she could hide. She took advantage of it and leaped over just as the lazarus ran passed her smashing right through the wall that had the Incubus' face embedded.

When all was quiet, she walked over to the hole to see an empty space. There were no other tunnels on the other side, it was empty and black. The hole slowly began to close like her bleeding hand from the knife. The daunting question in her mind emerged; was this a dream?

Tammra led Greg into a room while they continued to kiss and touch each other's bodies. Suddenly, they were taking their clothes off and crawled into the white bed with matching covers. Greg looked at her and she smiled back, "I want to feel you inside me," Tammra whispered.

Minutes turned into an hour and they were all sweaty while grinding their bodies together in love making that was like no other. When it was all over they laid in bed next to each other for a while and Greg looked at her.

"You were great," he whispered and got up to put his

pants on.

"No, no, you were great," Tammra insisted.

"What do you mean?" he asked.

"It means you were a great fuck. That's what it means, or need you forget that is what you like to play, right?"

Greg couldn't believe what he was hearing. Normally he took advantage of the girl, but this time it was he who was taken advantage of.

"I know all about your secrets," smiled Tammra with a sweaty grin on her face. "I know what you do to all the girls after you're finished fucking them. So I ask, how does it feel?"

"I'm getting out of here," said Greg as he kneeled down to tie his shoes.

"Better yet, how does it feel to be tricked and lied to?" said a rough voice. Greg looked up and saw that it wasn't Tammra, but Shanga. Shanga smiled and laughed at him.

"That's what I call fucking with your mind!" she snarled. Greg's eyes opened wide as he fell backwards while hearing her high pitch screech. He turned around and ran out the door.

Tammra walked around endlessly with no success. There were no windows and clues for that matter. She was running out of hope for escape and was just going to turn around when she came to an unfamiliar path. The teenager was now lost and getting angry. She continued to walk and looked carefully at all the paths around, but they went straight into infinity. Tammra began walking faster to make up for the time that was lost and felt tormented.

Eddie and the shadow continued to take drags and talk about life in general.

"I don't know what to think about life. I think it's a big joke, parents and teachers keep brainwashing us to believe we need to go to college or have some socialism and I think it's bullshit," said Eddie.

"If you hate life so much why not kill yourself?" asked the shadow. Eddie shook his head, "I don't know? Maybe I should, but I like to get high and have sex," he answered while picking up the pot leaves.

"Why do you serve the Incubus?" he asked as he turned around, but found Ezela was gone.

Tammra continued to walk around the hallways and couldn't believe she was lost. She began whimpering like a little lost puppy and remembered the time when she was a little girl and got lost in the super market. Except this was different, she just turned sixteen and was beyond in maturity. The only thing that was on her mind besides adulthood was the fear of getting raped. It was the fear that struck her when she was thirteen years old. An older man tried to rape her on her way home from school.

Tammra flushed it out of her mind and began thinking of Greg and how sexy he looked. She could endure the dirty sex, but it was the feeling of being used that was unappealing. Tammra continued to walk through the halls fantasizing about hot sweaty sex when something pulled her into a room. She opened her eyes and saw it was Greg and he looked nervous.

As she was just about to speak Greg covered her mouth, "quiet."

She looked from the corner of her eye and saw a group of shadows and decibels. After they passed, Greg retracted his hand away from her mouth, "I think our time is up." Tammra looked at him confused and realized what he was talking about.

"You mean the Incubus is already looking for us?" she asked as he nodded.

"I'm sorry we're going to be victims and if this is going to be the end I want you to know that I've admired your strength."

Tammra smiled and realized he was in love with her. She held his hand as the two made there way around the group of decibels and shadows to look for Shannon. Tammra was thinking about sex and her desire was to wrap her legs around his body to feel him inside her.

Then it happened, he kissed her and the two were over each other like crazy. She touched his strong arms and felt safe as well as secure. Greg turned her around while touching the middle of her spine and resumed tracing his lips over Tammra's shoulders. The hallway was empty and she felt Greg's strong hands begin to remove her clothes. His sensual lips could be felt all over the back of her neck and shoulders. Tammra was faced forward and enjoying his tender touch along her naked body. A cool draft of air touched her skin as she begged for more.
Suddenly, something cold and wet slid in her vagina and in between her legs. It was so big that that she screamed with excitement. He kept pushing further and she didn't know how to take it. Then she heard the sound of a clock ticking and then an unfamiliar voice bellowing in her ears, "how do you like that bitch! You love it don't you!"

Tammra turned her head and screamed at the sight of the Incubus's decibel, Tick Tock. Her beautiful moment of love was twisted into a never ending rape. Minutes turned to hours and she was sweaty, but then he removed himself from inside her and then went through her anus. She squealed because it was so big and was trying to escape, but couldn't break free because he had his big hands over her buttocks and waist.

"You like getting raped!" bellowed Tick Tock as he rotated from both gorges. Tammra suddenly began puking out white liquid from her mouth and her eyes flickered back from dehydration. All of a sudden she was thrown to the ground and turned her head to see the decibel look at her. Tammra's mouth opened wide when she saw his cock was a foot long and the diameter of a soda pop can. He threw her clothes at her, "get dressed you little whore, you're about to join your friends!" ordered the decibel as he left her there.

Tammra picked up her clothes slowly while crying as she felt a lot of pain in her vagina and anus. A flash back entered the teenager's mind of when she was thirteen and got raped. Tick Tock embedded the feeling in her mind that she was nothing, but a cheap whore and deserved to get raped.

Shannon ran through the tunnels until she finally got to the spot where they had all separated to find a way out. She found Eddie was already there with a big joint in his hand.

"Oh, hi Shannon," he smiled as he exhaled a gust of smoke in her face. Shannon began coughing and looked at him concerned, "where did you get that?" she asked.

Eddie grinned at her, "my new friend gave it to me. Pretty cool isn't it?"

"Oh, you're cool Eddie," replied Shannon sarcastically as she could tell he was stoned and had no idea what he was doing.

Greg emerged from the staircase and looked like he had just seen a ghost. He was so pale and scared. There was a sweaty odor that Shannon could smell from him and right away she knew something happened.

"Well, did you find anything that could help get us out of here?" asked Shannon. Greg shook his head, "no I couldn't find any clues."

Shannon looked at him concerned and wondered what had happened. He was avoiding eye contact as well as being short in conversation and he smelled like sex.

"Is there something wrong Greg?" she asked while touching him on the shoulder. He jumped up in the air, "don't touch me!" he exclaimed.

The Temple of the Incubus

"Oh my God, where did you go and what did you do?" She asked and felt goose bumps cover her body.

"Look, can we just get the hell out of here!" he exclaimed as he and Shannon saw Tammra.

Tammra was walking strangely and looked like she was in a lot of pain. The teenager didn't have much to say since she had just been raped. Shannon noticed the similar stench on her that was on Greg. Tammra's hair was also a mess and her eyeliner was smeared on her cheeks as though she had been crying. She looked like total crap and Shannon intuitively knew that her best friend had been raped.

"Tammra," Shannon smiled as she ran over to her and gave her a hug, but felt something was wrong.

"What's wrong?" she asked as she saw Tammra remained speechless and didn't want to talk about her rape.

"Tammra its me, Shannon!"

"Yes I know," Tammra replied as her eyes welled up with tears and began crying.

"What happened?" asked Shannon, but Tammra shook her head.

"I want to go home!"

"Did you find anything that would help us escape?" asked Shannon.

Tammra shook her head, "no I didn't find anything." Shannon looked at Tammra and was trying to figure her out, but couldn't. It was like someone put a black cloak over her best friend and nobody could see Tammra.

"Well," began Shannon as she looked at Greg and Eddie. "While you guys were out looking for an escape I came across something very unpleasant. I found a picture graph on the wall that I interpreted as Egyptian and a way out. If we are to escape we must try to find the silver mirror. That will enable us to escape from the temple."

"What do you know about that shit?" asked Eddie. "I learned it from school and the Discovery Channel. You know I am smart, I'm not a dumb blonde," replied Shannon.

"I don't want to leave," replied Eddie.

Shannon looked at Eddie very strangely and felt a great weight of evil creep from his brown eyes, "what are you talking about?" she asked.

"I found a room full of pot. If I play my cards right I can make more money selling weed than doing anything else," he smiled.

The Temple of the Incubus

"Eddie try to understand. The Incubus is using your fucking mind!" exclaimed Shannon.

"That's where you're wrong," yelled Eddie.

"My new friend Ezela promised me that I have nothing to worry about. You guys are the ones who are going to end up dead. Ezela is going to help me sell this shit and make a fortune," he boasted.

"What makes you think the Incubus is promising to let you live when I feel like he can come out and attack us at any given time!" yelled Tammra.

Shannon knew that when she saw the Incubus' face in the wall, he was already causing mischief. This could be one of them, to turn them against each other.

"She's right," agreed Greg as he heard the whispers from the women that he used for sex. *"Why did you hurt me Greg!!"* he heard one of them scream at him. Pictures emerged in his mind of hot sweaty sex with all of the girls he took advantage of. Their faces filled the mirror as they came out to attack him for the pain he put upon them. He saw himself at eighty years old, single, unhappy and miserable because no woman wanted him on account of what he had done. Greg tried to shake the guilt and the thoughts from keeping him focused on the escape from the temple. Tammra looked at him very concerned and wondered what was wrong. Shannon knew something happened to her best friend and classmates, but didn't know the details of what it was.

"I think the next step is to find the mirror or clear glass wall. It may be our only hope."

"Well, you can do it on your own. I'm staying here," replied Eddie.

"You son of a bitch you're backing out on us to help yourself!" exclaimed Greg.

"Yeah, well if the situation was reversed and there were hundreds of women in a room waiting for you, you would do the same thing! Am I right?" asked Eddie.

Greg didn't need to hear it, he had enough problems. The voices persisted and now his best friend was telling him that if there was something that he enjoyed he would be staying here as well.

"I have an idea," said Shannon as she watched the senior and junior get into a fight.

"Guys, guys, break it up!" yelled Shannon as she stood in between them. Eddie will you come along with us and help us escape?" asked Shannon.

The Temple of the Incubus

Eddie nodded, "I'll go along with that. Just keep that psycho away from me!"

Shannon turned to Greg, "do you think you can keep yourself under control long enough to escape?" Greg nodded and took a deep breath, "I think so," he answered as he took deep breaths to calm down.

They walked together as one, they weren't going to be separated again. Shannon led them to where she thought was a suitable place to look for clues. Eddie walked up beside Shannon to stay away from Greg. He was afraid that if Greg took the rear; Greg would take a swing at him for the cheap insult. Greg turned his head to glare at Eddie and wanted to kill him.

The Incubus had plans for this and wanted the teenagers to turn on each other. That was what the Incubus lived for, making people miserable and hateful. Tammra tapped Greg on the shoulder and smiled when he turned around to see her. Greg smiled back, but it was a fragile smile

"Can I talk to you about something?" she asked.

"Sure," he replied as he looked ashamed for thinking about taking advantage of her earlier.

"When you were out looking for clues did you notice anything really weird?" Greg looked at her concerned. "You mean anything of great consequence? Yes, I have been having these strange revelations of hearing and seeing women that I had gone out with a long time ago.

"And what happened?" asked Tammra.

"I didn't love them like I should've. I used them for sex."

"Then did you suffer from a fear or a sin?"

"I was used by somebody that I thought I knew well."

"Did she look like me?" asked Tammra.

"How did you know that?" he asked.

"I know this because I had what you could call an attraction to the kind of guy I wanted and somehow this place could read my mind like a book and fit everything out to the last detail. It's like this place can manifest all our fears and all our fantasies to become real," replied Tammra.

"Then what does the Incubus plan to do with Eddie?" asked Greg.

"I wish I knew? He is involved in drugs and must be selling his soul to the devil."

Greg looked at Tammra wondering what pain she had to pay in respects to her fantasies. "What did you have to suffer from, fear or sin?" asked Greg. Tammra looked at him as though she was afraid to answer.

"Fear," she answered.

"As an average girl I have been interested in guys, but I have had the fear of being raped and somehow the Incubus found out and was able to show me something that I wanted to see and feel something that I didn't want to feel."

"Did this guy who raped you look like me?" asked Greg. Tammra was quiet as though hesitant to speak.

"Yes," she whispered and nodded her head. Greg closed his eyes as though he couldn't believe this was happening. "There has got to be a way to kill this guy."

"He's not a guy. He's a demon," replied Tammra.

The group came to a halt when they came across an endless pit that opened and closed. It was eight by ten feet and closed itself shut and when it opened, it took up all the space in the hallway so they couldn't pass. Shannon counted how many seconds in between while it opened and closed to eight second intervals. She turned around to look at her friends.

"Ok we're going to run and jump while it's closing and keep running for another six feet so we won't fall through. Does anybody know what I'm talking about?" asked Shannon as she noticed there were no questions and every one nodded.

"I'll go first," she insisted.

Shannon began to run as the hole closed and she jumped. She flew through the air and over the opening area that was the danger. When her feet touched the floor there was a sigh of relief and she turned around to see her class mates look at her as the hole in the floor re-opened again and then close. Tammra charged quickly and ignored the pain in her vagina and anus. The hole began to close and she leaped, hoping that she would make it. She made it and the two girls took a look back at the guys. Greg had already began running and leaped as the chasm opened.

Shannon thought that Greg wasn't going to make it. She was proved wrong by the laws of physics that he would make it. His foot touched the floor just a couple of inches away from the opening of the hole.

"Are you crazy? You almost got yourself killed!" exclaimed Tammra.

"I made it, didn't I!" he declared.

"Never mind that," replied Shannon as she gestured Eddie to jump. Eddie began running and proceeded to jump as the opening closed, but the opening stayed open this time.

"Eddie!" exclaimed Shannon as she, Greg and Tammra ran to the edge of the pit to help him. Eddie flew through the air and reached his hands forward for help. The girls and Greg grabbed his arms as they felt an adrenaline rush through their bodies. The three of them struggled to pull him up out of the pit. This was hard because there was no way to get good leverage along the slippery smooth floor, but they managed to pull him up.

"Thank you," he replied.

Greg looked at him with very little respect, "you're welcome."

"If you are on the good list with the Incubus then why does he want to kill you?" asked Shannon.

Eddie shrugged as he was finally realizing that the Incubus didn't care if you were interested in staying and becoming part of the temple in human form. Eddie now knew that he was better off staying at home smoking pot or getting hauled in by the cops for illegal possession of Cocaine. Anything was better than staying here in the temple of the Incubus. Eddie felt betrayed and his true friends had just saved him from becoming devoured.

"I'm sorry for being a jerk," apologized Eddie.

"We learn from our mistakes," smiled Shannon. "Sometimes the hard way."

The situation became desperate as the thirteenth hour came close. It was like the eclipse of the sun before the apocalypse. It appeared there was no hope for escape and Shannon could see the emotional frustration in her friends. For Shannon it was either escape or die trying, but morale was low from the other three teenagers. They kept walking and hoped that this magical silver mirror that Shannon talked about so valiantly would pop up. Tammra stopped and looked around at the dirty pictures of the Incubus and his followers ripping body parts from humans. There were pictures of them having sex with men and women while they were being ripped apart.

"I can't stand it anymore," she complained as she watched Shannon stop and walk over to comfort her.

"I want to kill myself right now," cried Tammra.

"Why?" asked Shannon.

"We're never going to escape Shannon! This sick psycho is going to kill us the way the paintings on the walls show. I would rather kill myself than die this way!" sobbed Tammra.

"Tammra, we're going to escape. I need you to calm

down and help us find the magic mirror."

"Magic Mirror, what kind of crock of shit is that! This isn't Alice in Wonderland! I was raped by one of them! I had a giant penis inside me. The cock was so big that it hurt me and I don't want to be raped again. It felt agonizing and I would rather die than to have it inside of me again."

They suddenly looked around as the lights began to flicker the same as they did with Shannon. "Something's very weird here," said Tammra as she dried her eyes.

"What's going on?" asked Greg.

Shannon walked past Tammra and looked in the distance to see it was the lazarus and they were running in their direction.

"Run!" yelled Shannon as she began running away. Tammra squinted her eyes in the distance to see the animal like shadows squeal, grunt and scream in the corridor.

"What the hell is that!" Tammra yelled as she began running away and caught up with the others.

The lazarus were gaining on them and soon were right behind the teenagers.

They ran all the way to the end of the hallway until they came to an open chamber about the size of the high school gym.

"Oh no," murmured Shannon.

"Did we take a wrong turn?" asked Greg as he heard his echo throughout the gymnasium until he saw what Shannon saw.

"Oh shit!" exclaimed Tammra who was just behind them and screamed her head off.

It was the Incubus with hundreds of shadows and decibels. He was sitting in his throne, which was raised on top of a small pyramid of stairs made of gold, similar to the chest that brought them here. The chamber had black material hanging on the walls. Hundreds of the decibel and shadows were sitting on the floor cross legged.

Two decibels with long spears walked towards them and poked at the teenagers to come to their leader. The Incubus was smiling and looked like he was expecting them to give up.

"This wasn't a fair chance for our escape!" yelled Shannon.

The Incubus sneered, but said nothing since he was running the show. "I don't think you realize how generous I have been for not killing you quickly!" said the Incubus in his usual devilish voice.

"Then why didn't you kill us quickly? It sure beats killing us slowly so we can feel the pain?" demanded Shannon. Just then the lazarus came walking through from behind the teenagers to join them.

"You know what! I think I'll do that!" yelled the Incubus with a smile while pointing at Eddie.

All of a sudden, Eddie began coughing and convulsions occurred that caused him to not be able to breathe. The Incubus continued to laugh and then ceased, "people who do drugs should think about the consequences of what they will never be able to do for the rest of their life, such as, for instance, breathe."

Eddie vomited non stop and realized that what he smoked was not pot at all, but a plant that liquified his lungs and was killing him slowly. His throat burned and his eyes turned red and watery while veins began to pop out of his head. He was slowly puking out his lungs and little by little he was running out of time to live.

"Eddie," screamed Tammra and Shannon.

"Stop this!" exclaimed Greg, but it was too late Eddie was dead and his head dropped in his own puke.

Greg was in shock and the girls were crying. They knew Eddie for a long time and now he was dead. "You son of bitch!" exclaimed Greg. "Why don't you come down here and fight me. Do you know what I think when someone doesn't fight me man to man? I think the person is a real pussy."

The Incubus looked at him and was silent for a minute before he broke into laughter. The shadows, decibels and lazarus laughed with him as they stared at Greg. Shannon and Tammra looked at each other. "I don't like this," replied Tammra.

After the Incubus finished laughing he pointed at Greg. "You should be worried about your own fate and what I have in store for you because you're next on my list!" Greg felt shivers down his spine after the Incubus said that.

"So you're going to face me man to man?" asked Greg.

"Face yourself, woman to man you walking hormone!"

Greg suddenly fell through the floor where a pit opened up. Shannon and Tammra looked down the pit and saw Greg getting raped by an endless number of shadows. Greg screamed for help as they had their way with him.

Shannon wasted no time; she grabbed Tammra's hand and ran out of the open area they entered.

"Shannon we can't just leave Greg and Eddie here to die!" exclaimed Tammra.

"Believe me when I say this, they're already dead and

we're next if we don't leave!"

The Incubus realized that the girls were gone and looked at Tick Tock with a smile, "they're yours, but don't harm Shannon, she's mine." The Incubus sat in his chair, "kill the other blonde after you rape her." Tick Tock sneered and ran down the pyramid throne and shouted, "after those bitches!"

Shannon and Tammra ran through the corridors to lose them. They jumped over endless pits, past flame throwers, and ceiling traps from above. It was an endless run for their life.

"Shannon, I can't run anymore."

"We've got to or we'll never make it!" exclaimed Shannon.

"I can't, let's stop for a minute to catch our breath," replied Tammra.

Shannon turned around to see hundreds of decibels and shadows running in their direction. Shannon grabbed Tammra's hand, "come on, let's go!" she exclaimed.

Tammra turned around to see what was chasing them and screamed. All of a sudden she heard the sound of a clock and then something grabbed her legs and thrust her down to the ground like a dog. Shannon lost her grip and heard a terrified screaming coming from Tammra. Shannon turned to see Tick Tock trying to rape her best friend.

"Run Shannon run!" screamed Tammra as she felt Tick Tock rock her back and forth. The decibel was drooling and ripping her clothes off as her whole body slowly began turning into glass beginning with her hands and feet.

The decibel ripped the rest of Tammra's clothes off and was going to screw her like a dog. She felt something big and cold enter inside her already sore vagina, as large hands embraced her butt cheeks. Tammra started to cry as she began to turn into glass. Tammra was crying as the memories emerged such mind of when she was raped as a thirteen year old girl. Her arms and legs felt numb the glass began to cover those areas.

"No, please don't do this," she cried. "I'll do anything you ask, just please no more sex, I'm in so much pain," Tammra begged.

"Oh yes, you know you want it," roared the decibel as he laughed and shoved his huge drill in and out of her.

The lazarus, shadows and decibels ran past him to pursue Shannon. Shannon was far ahead and wasn't going to give in to failure. Shannon would rather die than to marry a freak of nature that was so demented.

"No" she screamed as he rocked her back and forth, faster and faster and let out a roar for everyone to watch. Then after the girl was completely turned into glass she shattered before busting into a million pieces.

Shannon didn't know how she got here and with the evidence at hand felt that she was dreaming and thought about this while running through the hallway. This domain; this house, this temple of the Incubus for some reason limited her abilities to protect herself. The teenager's fantasies and fears were used against them in a very strong way to make them feel pleasure, guilt or pain. What was her fear? Shannon thought and realized what it was, which was failure. Shannon's fear was failure to fit in with her class mates, her mother, and fear of not being loved back by a man she would someday marry.

She began to remember all the things that woke her up in nightmares when she was a child, which were the boogey man, drowning, visits by strangers, embarrassments from school. The fear of falling from great heights was what woke her up as a little girl. Shannon saw these dreams in black and white, but she didn't know if the dream would repeat itself.

The teenager stopped running when she reached a bottomless pit that was just before her. She turned around to see the Incubus' associates running towards her from the distance. Shannon then turned back around to look at the pit opening and closing. She took a deep breath held on to the memories that were inside her head as a child with her mom. She embraced them as she closed her eyes and jumped into the pit. She could feel the cool air run through her face, hair and felt her body relax. She opened her eyes to see a black and white photo in the distance. It suddenly got bigger and she fell into it, a new world.

Shannon walked around the strange house that looked thirty years old. Everywhere she looked the scenery was black and white with no other color which made her feel uneasy. There was a mirror on the wall and Shannon saw that even she was black and white. It was creepy and she didn't like being there at all, but continued to explore the house. Then the teenager heard a voice that sounded like her mother and decided to see if it was her mother. She walked down a short hallway and it got louder. Shannon pressed her ear against the door and heard a woman talking, "oh my baby girl, you're so beautiful."

Shannon opened the door slowly and peered in to see it was a young lady who looked like her mother. Shannon closed her eyes and reopened them with the slow shake of her head as though she couldn't believe what she was seeing. The lady in the room holding the baby was her mother and she looked at Shannon with a smile.

"Well hello there," she said.

"Hello," answered Shannon as she saw a different side of her mother.

She was dressed in her white night gown and her hair was long with white to signify the blonde that was in her hair. Shannon began to smile as she saw the baby that was about a year old. Shannon realized that the baby was her, then there was a flash of light.

Shannon looked around the black and white world to see the commotion of kids walking around with trapper keepers, books and notebooks. She was at her school and everything was black and white. Then she bumped into someone from behind and turned around to see a familiar face. It was Tammra and Shannon almost cried as she saw her best friend.

"Shannon, you better hurry to get to your English Class or you won't pass eighth grade.

Tammra gave Shannon a look with slang as she held her mouth open with a half smile. Shannon began to laugh as she remembered those days and remembered how Tammra looked as a freshman. They were always giving each other a hard time about the retro boring classes of junior high.

Tammra left to get to class so she wouldn't be tardy and Shannon tried to think what her class was like in eighth grade. She barely remembered what her locker number was and before she walked to her locker she met a familiar face, it was Michael. Shannon couldn't believe it was him and felt very strange.

"Hey," he said

"Hi," she answered as she saw how he was dressed and he parted his black hair.

"I wanted to know if you would go out with me?" he asked and smiled.

Shannon smiled and her heart melted as she realized this was the man of her dreams and this was when he had asked her out. He was just a little taller than she was and who knows what the future would hold for them. For all she knew they would be a romantic couple until they graduated and get married. How romantic, she thought and hoped that it wouldn't end the way it did before.

"Ok," she smiled and gave him her phone number.

He smiled and put the phone number in his wallet. Shannon saw the piece of paper and felt a burst of excitement enter her body. He put her phone number in his wallet and wanted her in his life.

"I'll call you tonight after school so we can take a stroll in the park and get to know each other better."

"Sounds like fun," replied Shannon and he smiled before leaving.

Shannon hesitated for a minute as she tried to think about this whole situation. She didn't know if she went back in time to relive the romance with Michael or rehearse the torture of being known as a whore. She tried to think about how she got here, but couldn't remember. Then there was a burst of light that encompassed the hallway and took her away from her black and white world.

The teenager opened her eyes and found herself in her room and saw the black and white photo of her mom holding a baby. The baby was a year old and brought shivers up and down her spine. Shannon got out of bed and realized that everything was in black and white. She walked to the door and opened it to figure out where she was. She peered down the hall to see a long white hallway with white doors that had golden door knobs. Shannon walked down the hallway and saw all the doors were closed.

Shannon suddenly began hearing light noises that were described as moaning from men and women. At first, Shannon began to smile as she imagined her first night with Michael. They could fulfill the experience of losing their virginity. She could already feel her body getting hot and sweaty. The teenager didn't want to be ashamed for thinking about it and doing it, so it would have to be a secret. A secret from her mother and the world.

The teenager heard the sound of screaming with excitement and then it grew quiet with more moaning. Shannon opened the door on the right and followed the short hallway in the small apartment in the black and white dream. The screams and moaning persisted until she came to the bedroom door. She took a deep breath and opened it to see two people having sex. To her surprise it was her and Michael, but before she could say a word they disappeared out of thin air, like a mist. Then there was a burst of light and she found herself somewhere else.

The Temple of the Incubus

Shannon was in a church and looked at herself in a white wedding dress, the symbol for virginity, purity and fertility. She looked around to see everything was in black and white just like an old film in the nineteen-fifties. The teenager turned her attention to the maid of honor, Tammra. Of course, Tammra looked much older and so did Shannon as she looked into a giant silver mirror with a silver stand.

"Are you ready for your big day?" she asked.

Shannon hesitated at first, "big day?"

"Yes, you're getting married to Michael," smiled Tammra as she continued.

"It's only been ten years since you graduated high school together. It was so romantic how he begged you back and now you're getting married."

After all was well Shannon walked down the long aile and saw the room was packed with people. Some of the people she didn't know and others were recognizable from childhood. In the distance she saw a man with short black hair faced away from her and Tammra smiling as she nodded her head. Then before she got five more steps there was a burst of light that shifted her mind to another life.

Shannon watched her mom tickle the baby that presumably was her. Sharon raised her daughter to the ceiling and kissed the baby on the lips when she lowered her down. Shannon began to smile and weep because she couldn't remember the last time they had that kind of relationship.

"Yes, you're a beautiful baby girl, someday you'll grow up to be just like me," said her mother as she smiled and made the baby laugh.

Ironically Shannon could remember when she was six years old telling her mom that she wanted to be just like her when she grew up. She would dress up like mommy and imitate the way she would talk to other people. She was a miniature Sharon, but what happened? Shannon thought as she touched the baby's head and felt its soft skin. Then there was a burst of light

Shannon rolled around the grass with Michael and they were laughing as they kissed each other. She could feel him kissing and sucking her neck and it was driving her crazy. It was such a good feeling to be loved by a man she felt was worthy to be hers. She touched his chest as he did the same and she began to get hot.

The Temple of the Incubus

Shannon touched his sweaty back with her hands and thought to herself; how would it feel to have him inside her? Then she felt sad when the time would come to face her mother about falling for her temptation for Michael. She would be whipped with shame and guilt for wanting to experience love. She was young, but Michael would wait for her because he loved her. The long wait would be worth it, but before she spoke there was a burst of light.

Shannon was in the hall way and continued to hear the loud orgasms. She walked over to the room with a door that was open a crack and walked in to see who was in there. It was an apartment and she followed it until she got to the bedroom and opened it to see two people under the blankets move. Shannon just knew that Michael was having an affair on her and tears began to emerge in her eyes as light filled the black and white room. A flash of light emerged to heal the pain in such heart to unveil another life.

The walk to the priest was like a symphony as she heard the sound of piano playing. She was almost to the alter, ready to stand next to Michael, the man deemed worthy of her love. Shannon realized that there was a problem when she noticed he was turned away, hiding his face, as though he was guilty. Then there was another burst of light that flashed before her eyes.

Shannon smiled after she touched the baby's head. The baby's head was soft with tiny facial features that were remarkable. Shannon dreamed of having a baby someday, a bundle of joy that would fill her life with such delight. Then Sharon brought the baby to her face and began blowing on her stomach while the baby began squealing with laughter. Shannon began to laugh as she remembered her mom doing that to her when she was a girl.

"So what's your name?" asked Sharon.

"Shannon."

"Oh my God, that's what I named my angel!" laughed Sharon excitedly as she played with the baby. "Do you want to hold her?"

"Sure," said Shannon as she noticed the black and white had turned to color and the teenager felt a light buzz on her neck.

Shannon held the baby gently in her hands and then suddenly the baby began growing bigger and bigger until she was about five years old. The resemblance was striking, a miniature

The Temple of the Incubus

Shannon, and Shannon stood up on her feet. She looked at her mother who was also standing up.

"You can drop her," said Sharon in a deep masculine voice.

"Drop her?" asked Shannon as she looked at her mother with a peculiar look.

"I dropped you when you were a baby, that's why you're so fucked up!" exclaimed Sharon as her eyes got sucked inside her eye sockets.

Shannon looked down and saw the child she was holding was a shadow with its body turned inside out. Immediately Shannon screamed her head off and then turned her head to who she thought was her mother, but it wasn't her mother, it was the Incubus. Shannon's vocal cords unleashed such a terrified scream that it would wake up the dead. She screamed again and a burst of light sheltered such mind.

The two teenagers were in the park kissing and everybody was gone. Shannon smiled at Michael and he unbuttoned her pants and put his hand inside. She began to breath deeply and realized she didn't want to do this anymore because of where it was leading. For her, it was like a flower growing from the ground and opening up its pedals to the first bee that came along and then dying after it gave itself away. She wanted it to be perfect and what better way than looking forward to the moment at a later date.

"What's the matter?" he asked.

Shannon took a deep breath, "I don't want to do this."

"What? Why?" he asked as he got up to his feet. "We talked about this and I waited all summer to show how much I love you."

"I know," she said as she buttoned up her pants and got up. "I'm sorry for leading you on like this, but I want to wait until I get married. I'm not like other girls, I want to be surprised and I want to feel like I earned it."

Michael looked disappointed at her and then turned away. Shannon never saw this side of him before and wondered what the big deal was. The scenery suddenly changed from black and white to color and Shannon looked around as she noticed the change. She touched Michael's shoulder and he turned around to reveal his face as the Incubus.

Shannon let out a scream and stumbled backwards as he got on top of her. A sweet innocent girl who was all alone in a park should have thought twice before being with a guy who only wanted sex with her. Claws began emerging from his fingers as he ripped her pants apart. Shannon began screaming even louder, "stop, stop this now!" she exclaimed.

The Incubus began laughing, "you're so sweet and tender! Everybody will think you're a whore if I don't do it."

Shannon let out another scream as she felt something enter inside her and a burst of light took shape.

The teenage girl looked at the sheets that were moving and saw movement on the top. She assumed it was Michael having sex with a girl, but Shannon couldn't see who it was. Then she heard a girl who sounded like Tammra start talking, "oh my God, you can ride me like a horse and fuck my brains out!" the sheets came off and Shannon's eyes opened wide. It was the Incubus and her girlfriend Tammra all sweaty with blood near her navel. The black and white changed to color and Shannon looked around the room, noticing the changes. She looked at Tammra and blinked with a surprise as the Incubus turned his head as well with Tammra's intestines in his mouth. He was having sexual intercourse with Tammra while he was eating her intestines from the open cut near her navel.

"Shannon its ok," assured Tammra as she watched Shannon kneel down and puke all over the carpet. The Incubus pulled the top of Tammra's head off and began cutting out pieces of her brain with his long finger nails and eating her brain like it was candy.

"Shannon its ok, it only hurts a little," Tammra kept repeating as the Incubus got up and walked towards Shannon, "when I'm done with her you'll be next as the object of my sexual fantasy!" Shannon was sitting in her puke and screamed as loud as she could with saliva dripping from her lips and teeth. She felt the burning sensation in her throat from the vomit and the emotional pain in her chest. A light flashed emerged and took her away.

Shannon stood looking at Michael who was faced away from her and wondered what was going on. She looked around at the crowd of five-hundred people who were there to watch them tie the knot. They've been planning this day for a long time, but only now it seemed that Michael was getting cold feet.

Finally Michael turned around, but he was the Incubus and his black hair started growing long over his tuxedo. A wicked smile emerged on his face as he walked towards his bride. Shannon looked around to see the black and white begin to turn into color as tears filled such eyes to the tones of her flesh resonated from the candle light.

Shannon began to hyperventilate and then she screamed as loud as she knew possible. The teenager turned her head to see that all the people in the seats were the Incubus' decibels and shadows. She turned to see that Tammra was Ezela and Shanga was her mom. Tick Tock was the Incubus' best man and was rubbing his twelve inch shlong while he was smiling.

"We're finally one, my dear Shannon and I can't wait for our first night together," laughed the Incubus and everyone in the audience began to clap their hands and cheer. They were witnessing the Virgin Marriage for the leader of the temple, the temple of the Incubus. There was no burst of light and the doors of the church closed as the echoes of Shannon's terrified screams intensified. The girl felt her life close in around her and couldn't breathe.

Shannon woke up screaming as she rose up from her sweaty pillow. She jumped out of bed and fell forward on all fours as she puked on the carpet. She could feel the burning sensation in her anus as the vomit spilled from her mouth. Shannon sat up and wiped her lips from the drool of puke from her lips with a small towel and tried to think. She remembered bits and pieces of the nightmare and realized that she was home. Six months of nightmares were taking a toll on her and the last thing the teenager remembered was falling in a bottomless pit. There were black and white images in her head, but she couldn't make sense of them. She didn't believe in God, but she was thankful to be alive from a nightmare that seemed so real. Then the face of the Incubus emerged as the temple rummaged through her mind.

This was the sixth nightmare this week and they were getting worse. Shannon had read tons of information on dreams, asked a witch to cast a spell of protection, put up a dream catcher, asked Jesus and Mary for help, but they all failed. She turned her head to the statue of Mary and saw water coming down from her eyes. The painting of Jesus still had what looked like tears in the form of blood come down his cheeks. Shannon looked at the framed photo of her and her mom on the wall and knew that it was familiar to her from a dream or a dream of a dream. The cute baby was her when she was a year old and her mother looked so happy.

She checked the clock to see it was a few minutes after five in the morning. Her dark blue eyes turned to the most recent school picture of her in a soccer jersey with her team mates. The picture was on the dresser in a frame with soccer balls. She was younger, beautiful with long blonde hair that was quite often high lighted with blonde streaks. She didn't join soccer this year because of the stress from Michael and her mom. She felt strange as though she was reliving the morning, but pulled herself together.

Shannon got up from the carpet and walked over to the mirror to see how she looked. The troubled teen tried to remember the dream that scared her to death. As she crept closer to the mirror the girl noticed how much paler she looked from yesterday. Shannon felt like she was half dead and felt sticky from the sweat under her armpits, chest and legs. Her T-shirt and underpants were all wet and it was a disgusting feeling that she didn't want to endure any longer. Shannon wiped the sweat from her forehead with her hand and thought about the nightmare with the Incubus. She couldn't remember anything, but she knew it was real and while she was there she couldn't remember anything else.

She took a deep breath and turned around to her dresser. A change of clothes would do with a new attitude to begin the day. Shannon pulled out a pair of blue jeans and a red, long sleeve, shirt with the rest of her underwear. She began thinking about school and hoped that the clothes she picked wouldn't make the kids at school talk about how stupid she looked.

Shannon opened the door and looked around to see it was dark in the hallway. She was scared of the dark; since the nightmares of the Incubus persisted to take over her body and soul.

"Come on Shannon get it together," she whispered to herself.

Each step of the way she took deep breaths, but heard the Incubus whisper her name in the night, "I want to get inside you Shannon."

Then she saw the devil with the mask emerge in her mind with a squeal and snarl. Shannon jumped with the thought in mind and turned around, but saw nothing and realized it was a de javu. She didn't think she was going crazy and tried to think of what was going to happen next.

Once in the bathroom Shannon shut the door and took a deep breath as she walked over to turn on the shower. She adjusted the faucet to get the right temperature from the running water so she wouldn't get sculled.

She thought about the dreams and pieces came into her mind. She remembered some of the dreams. One of them about her mom and the truth was she missed the way things were. There was a dream about a baby and she was holding her. She smiled and began crying as wanted to be that baby and receive all that unconditional love.

Shannon was disappointed with her life and didn't know how she got here. She touched the tooth brush and the ointment as she looked at the mirror and felt like she already had done that. Then she remembered pieces of the dreams that she had with Michael. Of course Michael really did get mad at her when she refused him and spread terrible rumors that she was a whore. What about now and the future would they be together again?

One rumor was that she had crabs and herpes and another rumor was she had an abortion from a previous relationship. Many of the girls laughed and talked among themselves about her and singled Shannon out during social hours. Shannon thought about it a lot as she looked at her naked body and saw strange claw marks near her navel. Her lips began trembling as she tried to figure out how they got there.

She dared to dream and turned the CD player on as she slid a CD in by Knights and Banshees to a song that fit her mood for her ex-boyfriend, but then she stopped when she had another de ja vu of the song and picked a different song, which was left on repeat; *I'm Angry At You* ;

I'm angry at you
for the way you walk
for the way you talk
I'm angry at you
don't ask me why
I'll tell you to die
things just aren't
       so simple anymore

don't think about me
the way you see
it haunts my body for you to see
so don't try to understand
I'm angry at you
for all things you did
and I hate you for all your lies
playing games with my head
I wish you were dead
regretting what you said
while you don't even look in my eyes

The Temple of the Incubus

I'm angry at you
for all the things you said about me
behind my back
I'm angry at you
for the way you turn your back
on my innocence
I said
I'm angry at you

      The water ran hot on her face as steam filled the bathroom
and fogged up the mirror. Shannon closed her eyes and tried to
relax with the hot water hitting her breasts and running down to her
navel. Shannon's hair was wet with conditioner as she massaged
her scalp and moved down to her breasts with her hands.
      She remembered parts of the dream with Michael and it
had to do with rolling around on the grass kissing. It was fun and
romantic to feel so in love with a boy her own age that it made her
cry. She remembered all the fun they had going to the movies and
as funny as it sounded they made out most of the time. They never
could remember the movie because they were busy kissing and
touching each other.
      Then the fantasy emerged to make love with Michael.
She didn't care that she hated him for hurting her, but he was the
closest thing in her mind to fulfill such a fantasy. She imagined
him squeezing her breasts in the hot shower and taking deep
breaths while kissing her.
      "Oh Michael," she cried.
      She began touching herself between her legs when all of a
sudden Shannon felt pain. She opened her eyes and looked at
where the pain was and saw that she was bruised and inflamed.
She couldn't remember what happened and began wondering if she
was raped. The only one that could have raped her would have
been the Incubus. She looked at the wall of the shower and for a
split second saw the face of the Incubus laughing at her.
      "Shannon you've been in the shower for forty fricken
minutes. You're taking all the hot water!" exclaimed her mother
from outside the door.
      When she got out of the shower it was full of steam and
the feeling of unrest filled her with fear because the nightmares
had fog as well. The evil experience of the Incubus' appearance
emerged in her mind as she wiped the mirror with the towel. For a
split second she saw a mask and the face was laughing at her.
Shannon shrieked and then it was gone as she felt like she had

52

done this before. She continued listening to the heavy metal song that was on repeat and couldn't forget about what he had done to her. The teenager thought about this as she feathered the foundation and eye shadow around her eyes and face.

Shannon stopped what she was doing and looked at her fingers and the make up on the style that she used to put on her lips. It happened again and now it was obvious that she had already done this before, but what did it mean? Suddenly, she accidentally dropped her powder down the sealed sink and the powder turned into the shape of a mask. Shannon gasped and backed away, "oh my God, oh my God, oh my God."

Shannon walked back into her room with the cordless phone. Then she saw the puke on the carpet and realized she forgot all about it. She was all dressed up, her face full of make up and her hair blow dried, now she had to clean up her vomit. The teenager sulked and cleaned up the mess. She closed her door to keep the conversation private as she dialed Tammra's phone number and waited for her best friend to pick up.

"Hello," replied a tired voice.

"hi," said Shannon.

"Shannon?" asked Tammra, "what's going on?"

"I had that nightmare again with the Incubus," began Shannon.

"What?" asked Tammra.

"Yeah, that dream, you know, the one with the creep, who wears the mask and is chasing after me in the house. I'm really scared Tammra and I need someone to talk to," said Shannon.

"Oh my God Shannon, you'll never believe what happened to me? I went to a party last night at Greg's house and he invited me into his room and oh my God have I got a story to tell you!" screamed Tammra with excitement.

Shannon hesitated and felt like she already experienced this from Tammra and even if she didn't why was Tammra changing the subject? She couldn't put her finger on it, but she felt like her problems were not worth Tammra's time. Shannon felt the pain in her chest spread to her limbs as she heard her voice break when she spoke.

"I need someone to talk to and I don't want to talk about Greg. I don't care how much you desire him?" asked Shannon.

"I'm sorry, are you still thinking about Michael?" asked Tammra.

"Yes," answered Shannon. "I can't help it, I loved him

and gave him my heart. I feel a lot of pain because of what he did to me. Last night I had a bunch of nightmares and the Incubus was in them.

"Ok, I tell you what; I'll pick you up in my car and since today is skip day we'll do some catching up."

"Oh I can't skip today," said Shannon as she stopped and felt like she already experienced this strange phenomenon.

"Why not? Today is Friday! We got to catch up and talk about guys. We've been invited to a party today!" ordered Tammra.

"I'm sorry, but I'm not in the mood," replied Shannon.

"Ok, I guess I'll talk to you at seven, keep your chin up," answered Tammra.

"Ok, I'll see you soon," Shannon answered and hung up the phone.

The teenager thought about the pieces of her nightmares as well as the temple with Eddie puking his lungs out. Shannon began to sniffle, but she took a deep breath to keep herself from falling apart and thought about her mother and going down stairs to get ready for the day.

Shannon grabbed her head set and CD's; closed the door behind her as she walked into the kitchen and turned the coffee maker on. She went through the play list carefully selecting her band Slave Dancer as she clicked it to a song. The song was called My Aversion From You. The song reflected how she loved Michael, but was pushed away into an unknown realm of her life.

if words could carry metaphors
into the reality of a storm
we would live in a dark age like no other
you said you would be by my side
you lied to me, what is wrong with me?
is this the final end of what it should be?
I don't know why?

as a human I seek only answers
    to endless questions
I look up to the moon
    as a stranger with apprehension
I feel the wind blow
    my hair back as I stare
        at the veil shroud
I gasp for air

The Temple of the Incubus

            when I feel you kiss my neck
I turn around and there you are
I come from a town where everyone knows you yet I feel so far
you wave and blow a kiss good bye
            so very sad I bid fair-well

there in my kingdom I don't exist
you make your appearance
            in the image of a ghost
I tremble in shame
            as the wind hits the coast
I feel my veins turn into ice
            as I begin my aversion from you

      Shannon nodded her head up and down to the rhythm of
the song. The sad part of all this emotional wreck was that she
ignored a guy who was interested in her. She cut him down and
hurt him because she was hurt. As she cracked open a couple eggs
and put some bread in the toaster there was a pain in her chest, a
broken heart. Then a flash back entered her mind of when she was
a child and she wanted to be like her mom. She suddenly became
sad and began to cry, but she dried her eyes and realized she had to
make changes in her life.
      Before she knew it, it was a quarter to seven and she sat at
the table eating breakfast. The teenager thought about everything
in her life and the goals of what she wanted in her life. Shannon
looked at the picture of when she was a baby and her mom holding
her close. She took off the head set because her ears were hurting
and wiped her eyes from the tears that were shed.
      She sipped her coffee and then her mother was in the
kitchen. The tall, forty year old woman looked like an older
version of Shannon. Sharon looked as she usually did every
morning and quickly Shannon hid the framed photo on her lap. She
wanted to wait and hear what her mother would have to say, but
she predicted that it would be a bad morning.
      "You left the coffee pot running yesterday," she said.
      "Oh I did? I'm sorry it won't happen again," replied
Shannon.
      "Yes you did so don't do it again. I don't want my house
to burn down."
      Shannon hesitated as she tried to think about what to say.
      "Mom I've been doing a lot of thinking and I want to
improve my life. What can I do to improve?" she asked.

"Well you can start by not dressing like a slut and stop hanging around your slut friend."

Shannon began sulking, "oh my God here we go again."

The teenager continued to eat and thought about how to rectify the conversation Then again maybe it wouldn't be a bad idea to skip school and move on with her life. Nobody seemed to care about her troubled life or failing English class. Then her mom sat down across from her and Shannon watched the older woman drink her coffee.

"You know, our next door neighbor's kid who's the same age as you passed her SATS with a 133 score and there sending her to Harvard," began her mom.

Shannon felt the relapse of what was said as the tension began to build in her shoulders. She needed time to think about how to avoid this conflict and thought about pieces of the dream. Pieces of the dream emerged when she was a little girl and wanted to be like mommy.

"Did you know that your cousin Emily made the Dean's List," began her mother and smiled. "Emily's only a year younger than you are. Did you hear, she has the opportunity to get into any college?"

"That's good mother," answered Shannon.

"College is important, you can't roam around the country side for the rest of your life and hang around your slut friend."

"That's not very nice, mother."

"What's with the change in attitude you usually always fight to prove I'm wrong and your right."

"Maybe I don't feel like fighting," said Shannon.

"She's a slut and look at how she has you all dressed up. You look so skanky and sluty."

Shannon pulled out the picture of her as a baby with her mother and showed her mom the picture. Sharon looked at the picture as she drank the coffee in one gulp and set it down. Her mother looked at it and then at Shannon as though she didn't expect it and laid it flat on the table.

"It's a picture of you when I was born and when I was five years old I told you I wanted to be just like you," replied Shannon.

"Oh my God, I forgot about the little girl that you used to be," began her mother as she heard Shannon take a deep breath of relieve and smiled.

"You used to be so cute, so little and full of life," continued Sharon as she smiled.

The Temple of the Incubus

"I remember your first day of school to the first tooth lost and all the way up to the time you met you're friends who turned you into the girl you're now," answered her mother.

Shannon stopped smiling and felt something cold from the tone in her mother's voice. Her mother was warm when she saw the photo and seemed so happy when she saw the photo and then when the conversation ended with her as the girl she is now it sounded cold and bitter.

"Girls that go on the one way track to a slut never come out of it. They become a whore for life and they become pregnant at a young age with a bastard child. That's what you are and that's all you'll ever amount to," replied Sharon.

"But," Shannon began crying, "I want to change, I want to be like you."

"You could never be like me. Girls like Tammra and the girl that you are now can never go back to the way you were. You can only be one thing, a slut and later a whore after you've finished shagging dozens of boys at school and bare bastard children."

Suddenly Shannon got really pissed off and felt a huge adrenaline rush as she yelled, "you're a fucking bitch!"

"Don't you dare talk that way to me in my house!" exclaimed Shannon's mom.

"I try to open up to you and you slam the door in my face. Fuck you, you mother bitch!" yelled Shannon as she walked out and slammed the door in her mom's face.

The old Pontiac Sun Fire rolled up the black top driveway. Shannon ran out of the house looking upset and in tears. She slammed the door after getting into Tammra's car.

"Well, what are we waiting for? Lets go!" exclaimed Shannon.

"Shannon, what happened?" Shannon didn't answer so Tammra backed out of the driveway and peeled out with the music blasting.

I try to talk some heart
its very difficult for me
to tell her how I feel
when she doesn't shut the fuck up
I lose my direction
and I don't know where to start

The Temple of the Incubus

I can see her hoar
even after I'm out the door
I can smell her perfume
I can't stand the smell of whore
I hope one day the earth swallows her
mother bitch
mother bitch

I know its sad to say
people should know
what you see is what you get
don't be alone with what you fear
now that I know what she is

I can see her hoar
even after I'm out the door
I can smell her perfume
I can't stand the smell of whore
I know one day the world will swallow her
mother bitch
mother bitch

They were cruising in style with the music loud in the car. It was the band Knights and Banshees with the song Mother Bitch II. They were singing it on the way to school and getting their frustration out with the music.

Shannon took deep breaths as she looked through the window to see the houses pass by and realized that she was psychic. Any minute they would run into something rickety, old and spooky. She couldn't remember exactly what it was, but she knew that they would come upon it soon. Shannon turned her head to Tammra who was driving and turned her head to smile at Shannon. There didn't seem to be anything out of the ordinary with Tammra. She was the same girl that she knew from first grade. Maybe there was a way to avoid the temple and save her class mates. The two girls were best friends since Shannon was in kindergarten. She turned down the music and looked at Shannon who looked disturbed.

"What's the matter Shannon? You look like shit!"

Shannon raised her eyebrows, "my mom's a fucken bitch and I learned I'm psychic!"

The Temple of the Incubus

Tammra began to smile, "So were you like, struck by lightning or something? What were you and your mom fighting about?" she asked. Shannon looked at her best friend and didn't answer.

"Were you fighting over me?"

"I showed my mom a picture of me when I was a baby and told her I wanted to be like her after she criticized my intelligents by comparing me to my cousin and neighbor. She kept telling me I'm a slut and that's all I'll ever amount to anything. She said that I'll be a whore and end up as a pregnant teen with a bastard child," said Shannon as she began crying and tears began to fall down her cheeks.

Tammra began to sulk, "Oh my God, what a bitch."

"Aren't you still a virgin?" asked Tammra as Shannon sniffled and wiped her eyes.

"Well your mom obviously doesn't know you," continued Tammra. "Stick with me girl and you will go places," declared Tammra as she continued to watch the road and was about to turn the music back up when suddenly Shannon started talking.

"Promise you'll listen to me," said Shannon.

"Ok, what's the matter?" asked Tammra.

"I had a dream that you died. Two of our upper classmates died to, Eddie and Greg."

"Greg and Eddie?" asked Tammra. "This is one of your psychic predictions?"

"You could say that," replied Shannon.

"So tell me about your dream what happens to me and the guys?" began Tammra.

"You die," answered Shannon. "You die in the Incubus' temple."

Tammra rolled her curly blond hair over her right ear and looked into the rear view mirror. Shannon watched her look in the rear view mirror and knew that there were no cops. She looked a little bit uneasy to hear what Shannon was talking about. They had been through worse things in life, but nothing prepared Tammra for what Shannon had to say.

"There aren't any cops behind us," assured Shannon.

Tammra turned her head to Shannon and stammered, "how did you know I was looking for cops?"

Shannon ignored the question and asked, "aren't you going to tell me the reason I don't attract any guys is because I look like shit?"

Tammra didn't say anything and kept on driving. She was

thinking about these thoughts, but didn't say it out loud. The teenager was getting goose bumps from hearing these things.

"Next thing you'll say is how you compare sex to a Banana Split and that it isn't hard to get laid."

Tammra slammed on the breaks and pulled off to the side of the road, "what the fuck is going on? How did you know I was thinking those things?" demanded the teenager.

"I don't know how I know. I just know that I'm stuck in some sort of loop and everything is replaying out as before. I get pictures in my head of events and they come out in pieces that I can't explain. I tried to fight it and avoid the situations by reconnecting with my mother and it still went to shit."

"What is going to happen next that's going to be wrong?" asked Tammra, but she didn't get an answer to her question.

"I'm scared Tammra," began Shannon as she looked at Tammra and held her hand.

"What else are you scared of?" asked Tammra.

"The Incubus," answered Shannon.

"What?"

"I'm scared he'll take my virginity and use me to increase the size of his temple and go after other virgin girls. I'm scared I'll go through an endless life of being twisted inside out and raped over and over again.

"You said you had a dream of me being killed. Talk to me about the dream?"

Shannon looked at Tammra and was hesitant to talk about it. She felt awkward about sharing the dream, but Tammra was the only one there for her and deserved to know what was going on. Shannon took a deep breath and tried to think about the dream with Tammra. At first the dream came through really fast in pieces, but she was able to make sense of one of them and prepared to tell Tammra.

"Shannon, tell me what's going on in your dream," demanded Tammra as she watched Shannon lick her trembling lips and prepare to speak.

Shannon looked around the strange room she was in. The room was black and she was lying on a bed that was black as well with blankets to match. The walls were painted with a strange resin that looked like there were bones and bodies stuck in the wall. Shannon began to shriek at the sight of it and got up from the bed.

There was a strange eerie feeling she felt was invading. The corner of her eye caught movement in the walls. There were faces looking at her, but when she turned around to see what it was they were gone. It was only a figment of her imagination. Shannon felt the hair on the back of her neck stand up. The teenager walked over to the door and opened it to see what there was.

Shannon found herself in a long hallway with doors and behind each door she heard noises. The noises were the sound of men and women having sex. The sound of breathing polluted her ears as well as the high pitches of women having orgasms. Every step of the way the paces of screaming and breathing persisted.

All the doors were closed except one and she became interested in what was behind the door. There was screaming and shouting as a woman was having an orgasm. The teenager carefully slid open the door and walked in to see what was going on. She could see a short hallway with white paint and what looked like sun light coming in from windows that were draped.

Shannon could see there was a small kitchen and finally came across the living area. She saw a white bed with white blankets and a bed spread. By the way the blanket moved she knew that there were two people having sex, but then the blanket moved aside revealing who they were. Shannon was shocked to see Tammra naked and all sweaty with someone on top of her with long black hair. Shannon saw the man turn his head to face her and she realized that he was the Incubus. He rose up with Tammra's intestines inside his mouth. There was blood all over Tammra's chest and abdomen and the inside of the bed was red. He gobbled up the intestine like they were long loins of pork. He looked like he was wearing a mask that was attached to his face, but it was not a mask it was his face. He revealed an evil smile with sharp teeth and screeched, "Shannon I'll get inside you the way I got inside Tammra. You know you want me to."

Tammra stared at her best friend after hearing about the dream. Shannon looked scared and turned to stare at the window. The two friends were quiet until Tammra broke the silence, "wow, I don't know what to say."

The Temple of the Incubus

Shannon looked away from her best friend. Tammra could tell by the way Shannon turned away that she was ashamed and scared. What happened to Shannon? Tammra thought as she faced forward and scratched her nose. She never experienced this from her best friend who wanted to keep her virginity, something so unimportant to lose.

"I don't expect you to understand," replied Shannon.

"Shannon everything will be fine."

They continued driving through town and Tammra beeped her horn at two guys, Greg and Eddie. They were walking to school and Shannon saw them with something in their hands. They both were carrying a black chest that had gold trim around it.

"Oh my God, Oh my God," she repeated in a whisper.

"Hey you sluts, need a ride?" shouted Tammra as she laughed. Both of the guys smiled as they walked and got in the back seat.

"Are you fucking crazy? They're carrying the chest that was inside the house we broke into!" exclaimed Shannon.

"Is this another one of your psychic predictions? Shut up Shannon, maybe in your dreams you get trapped in your hamper, but this is reality." Greg and Eddie climbed in after opening the back doors, "are you guys skipping school to?" asked Tammra.

"Hell yeah, who cares about school, nobody gets anywhere with a diploma anyways. We've got enough stupid people in the world," laughed Eddie.

"Hey Shannon can you hold this?" asked Greg as he shoved the chest on Shannon's lap. Shannon looked at the object scared and began freaking out.

"Oh my God, Oh my God," she repeated as she stared at the key lock. It had the face of the Incubus staring at her with a demented smile. Shannon watched Greg and Tammra kissing in front of her. After a few minutes they stopped and when Shannon turned her head to Tammra they gave her a puzzled look and her best friend began to sigh. Greg whispered in Tammra's ear, "I can't wait until tonight."

Tammra smiled and kissed his neck, "just do me."

Shannon turned her head to the window as she heard a song by REVERSE and the lyrics stuck in her head like a bad dream. Tammra looked at Shannon and shifted the car in gear as she peeled out. Shannon felt an adrenaline rush and was scared.

The Temple of the Incubus

I'm bleeding through my eyes
all I see is red before me
I'm feeling empty inside
I have no tears to cry
I'm bleeding through my eyes
all I see is death before me
I'm feeling empty outside
and nobody knows why
I'm bleeding through my eyes
feeling my cornea peel open wide
screaming cries as they echo and die

everybody asks me what's it like
        to bleed through your eyes?
I tell them its like riding a bike
you get scraps and cuts
        but soon it dies
after the misery passes
        you grow numb and empty
you can feel it eat at you inside and out
feelings of sorrow
        and remorse are nothing
like the power of sympathy
you don't feel sorry
        for others or for yourself

you would ask me to hide myself
        but you're waiting to see
           what will happen next
you rancor this place
        that everyone calls life
         this living hell

       They were driving at high speeds of ninety miles an hour and Shannon felt petrified. The houses and cross streets were a blur as though she was spinning around in circles and she started getting dizzy. She felt that Tammra was not herself and knew something was wrong.

       "Slow down you're going to get us killed!" exclaimed Shannon.

       "You're the psychic what happens next?" began Tammra jokingly with a sneer.

The Temple of the Incubus

"I know what I'm doing. I just want to show you something," said Tammra as her voice became lower.

Tammra continued driving really fast in the car and was taking wild turns left and right to each cross street. Shannon could hear Eddie and Greg laughing and cheering about how happy they were. Shannon realized she was holding the chest in her hands and immediately rolled the window down and tossed it out.

"Hey, you fucking bitch, that was mine!" exclaimed Greg.

"No it wasn't," began Shannon as she turned her head at Tammra who gave her a strange look with the expression of why?

"It's evil and I'm not holding it."

All of a sudden they came across an old mysterious house on the driver's side. Shannon quickly looked at the house and opened her mouth with a gasp, "oh my God, this is the same house that's in my dream, only it's bigger!" she yelled.

"You've been to this house before?" asked Tammra.

"Not by choice, it haunts my dreams and inside of it is the Incubus," said Shannon.

"Let's check it out!" laughed Eddie.

Shannon got out of the car with the teenagers. They looked at the house and it looked like there was a lot of activity. There were bright lights coming out of the windows and a black storm above it with the sound of thunder and lightning striking the roof.

"Do you want to check it out?" asked Tammra. Shannon turned her head to look at her best friend suspiciously, "hell no!" answered Shannon as she heard a loud crackly sound of fireworks and looked to see the light show.

"Oh wow, that's so amazing!" laughed Tammra. "It's a celebration of the Virgin Marriage," replied Tammra. Suddenly Shannon heard a sound of a clock, tic tock tic tock and Shannon quickly turned around to see it was the Incubus' decibel Tick Tock with the shadows Ezela and Shanga.

"No!" screamed Shannon as she saw Tick Tock smiling at her with his large drill bit between his legs.

"What's the matter Shannon? We didn't come all this way for nothing," said Ezela. Shannon turned to run away, but Tick Tock grabbed the teenager and picked her up over his shoulder as the trio began walking to the house.

"Let me go you mother fuckers! Help, somebody help me," cried Shannon.

Then it occurred to her that she never left the temple. A

flash back entered her mind that the chest sucked the four of them inside the temple and that they were in another dimension. As she was carried back to the house Shannon was screaming her head off, begging for help and looked at all the houses with decibels picking up their mail and shadows tending their garden, even the children looked like them. Shannon realized that she was the virgin bride for the Incubus and would be living a life in the dream world of sex, pain and torment.

Tick Tock carried her inside the front door, but this time they walked through two doors into a huge gymnasium that looked like her old high school gym.

Shannon was squirming, hitting, crying and screaming as she saw all the shadows and decibels sitting in chairs and bleachers. Then when he set her down he watched her jump up and down like a little five year old, screaming her head off. She tried to escape, but the dark evil bodies prevented her from running away. She screamed some more and cried for help.

"Shut the fuck up!" shouted Tick Tock as he growled.

Shannon looked around and saw her mother there in human form just before she changed into a shadow. Then Shannon turned her head as her lips trembled and looked to her right, to see the Incubus standing next to her. He was dressed in a tuxedo and his hair was nicely combed.

"I told you we would be together," he said.

There was a huge cheer of applause from the audience as Shannon looked around and let out a huge scream. The scream echoed throughout the gymnasium and out the doors of the aile. Then the Incubus started laughing and the two doors slammed shut to keep the uninvited out from the Temple of the Incubus.

The chest was slammed shut and the dark stranger in the black trench coat relocked the chest. He looked around with his yellow eyes as he looked through his white albino hair. He smiled with his sharp crooked yellow teeth as he held the chest in his arms and left the old house. After he left and walked to the side walk, the house disappeared out of thin air, leaving it as an empty lot. The stranger walked towards the high school as he heard a car drive past with the music blaring and started to whistle the song he heard and said, "where else can I go that has teenagers, but a school with virgins."

The Temple of the Incubus

idiots
like you
deserve
the way
that you live
fools
like you
deserve
the hell
that you get

you are happy
that you got
what you deserve
you are crabby
that you got
what you preserve
you are crazy
that you lost
what you conserve

stolen hope
was all that you had
you had all that was given
and still you're unhappy
with what you have
you lay around the house
complaining about your life
you look around from being so sad
still you're staring at the wall
       waiting to be driven
and still you're unhappy
with what you had

idiots
like you
deserve
the way
that you live
idiots
like you
deserve
the hell that you bring

The Temple of the Incubus

idiots like you
deserve
the hell that you get

The Author's Thank You List

I would like to thank my sisters (my strongest support and inspiration); Ariane, Stephanie, Kayla, dad and mom. Special thanks to Debbie (I really appreciate your help, I couldn't have gotten this far without you) and Stan. I would also like to thank my grandma, aunts uncles and my cousins for your support. I would like to Thank Melissa and Maureen for reading my poems from "What I Think About You" and your supportive constructive criticism to continue to be creative. I would like to thank Kisus Metoxen (best friend and pen pal), Pam and Michelle Johnson of Lightning Source, Corinne (Cheetah) (for teaching and showing me what it means to give hugs and believe in your dreams), I would also like to thank my friends at Pizza Hut, and UPS for reading older versions of this story and inspiring me to keep going with it and my other books; Linda Mancheski(The best RGM manager I've ever had) , Marry and Marty Fagnan(for reading my works) , and Mike Van Ness (for telling me I've got a gift). I would also like to thank, Robert Harris (for getting me inspired in my first novel), Lisa Hildebrandt (for falling in love with me as a person and show interest in what I write), Mrs. Murphy (for encouraging me in writing), Lisa Steiner (for loving me even though I didn't do a good job at loving you back), Mr. Frautschi (believing I can do anything), Naomi Pidd (for the experience of waiting until you get married and reading my work), Mrs. Erickson (inspiring me with my novel), Mrs. Klass (for helping me succeed in my dreams and I have), Mary Olson (helping me find God and I found God in 2002), Alice Stout (being nice to me when nobody else was), Jeff Hanson (encouraging me to write music), Cheryl Boden (teaching me my sixth sense), Gabe Wahl (scaring the bullies away and being a friend), Duane Standard (helping and inspiring me to write and find romance), Duane Martinson (sitting next to me while I was writing my songs and encouraging me to write), Chris Lee (showing me how to draw Garfield in 2nd grade, which led to writing), Ms. Bongers (siding with me against the kids at school that would pick on me and encourage me to continue writing my novel), Mrs. Driscol (for telling a student to leave me alone who was picking on me and wouldn't leave me alone) Angie Rivard (a huge encouragement to accept who I am), Mr. Rivard (showing optimism in my strength in running and writing), Mrs. Quiling (letting me play all day and create), Mrs. Refsnyder (the best first grade teacher I've ever had), Mrs. Eck (showing me short cuts in learning), Jeff and Rob Pierson (Two brothers who made

me feel like a brother, thank you) , Ms. Morse, (for reading my novel) Mrs. Belisle (for reading my novel) Shannon Barkley (a good friend who gave me memorable experiences to write about), Deb Zeilsdorf (for making me laugh when I was down), Dave Hanson (for reading my stories and leading me to God) , Freddy Henzler (a huge inspiration for writing, drawing and seeing the good in everyone), Karin Dillner (making me laugh and feel special at "Arts World"), Stephanie Grimm (for inspiring me to illustrate and experience the attitude of someone young), Kathy Kleinhans, (for encouraging me to continue writing and to not stop) Cathy Garbe (for getting me interested in the writing school and giving me excellent feed back on my stories), Jeremy Gilbert (for your expertise to choose the right college that led to being more creative), Dave Herr (your encouragement to being creative), Darren Corbin (motivating me to go for my dreams), Mrs. Irlebeck (getting me interested in writing in 3rd grade), Dave Hunt, (for seeing me as the good person that I am as well as writing and one of the reason I joined basketball in 8th grade) Keith Moyer (for being my best friend in Junior High and part of high school and kicking *ss on TMNT Arcade), Craig Peterson (for encouraging me to continue writing), Darlyn Thomas (for your enlightenment to see that everyone is intelligent), Lori Johnson (for the article on publishing), Jay Fletch (for teaching me how to draw in 5th grade it really helped motivate me in writing), Trautmiller family; Freddy, Timmy and Matt (my neighbors) (had a lot of fun 4-wheeling, playing pool, fools ball, playing football, basketball, baseball and for Freddy who got me started on the first paragraph of my novel, thanks), Chad Hill (for being a good friend and influence), Robert Norton (for leading me to Kristy and telling me I need to write and get my stories published), Adrian Bravo (with his amazing illustrations), Trent Landry (for inspiring me to join Trek, but also that a man can accomplish anything when he tries hard enough) and the Landry family for visiting and supporting my last book signing.
I would like to thank my friends at McDonalds and Goodwill for your support in my dreams and everyone that was a huge influence, but aren't mentioned. You know who you are.

Artist I would like to thank that inspire me to write; Jane Siberry, Enya, Rummstein, Ozzy Ozbourne, KMFDM, NIN, Garbage Litta Ford, Within Temptation Epica, Nightwish and Mozart Celtic. I thank you.
I would like to thank my friends at the news paper; The

Hudson Star Observer, Doug Stoulberg, Julia from the New Richmond Paper, Erik from the Stillwater Gazette, Gary King of The Tri-County Paper and Norma from the Somerset Library.

This is a note for the jocks, popular kids, prissy preppy girls and drug attic bullies who picked on my sister (upperclassman and underclassman alike) for being a virgin for not being smart enough or good enough for you. She is good enough. This book was conceived and created based on my feelings towards those that bullied Ariane in junior high and high school to the point where she wanted to commit suicide. This book is not about giving you recognition or any encouragement for what you got away with, but the opposite. All the girls in my sister's class that ganged up on her in verbal, physical, mental abuse as well as ex-communicated and mis-treated her (you know who you are) are nothing but a bunch of cheap whores, sluts and expendable low lives. The guys who acted the same way are sub-humans, jack asses that have no brains, my pet dog was better than you. May you try to live a good life knowing that you are nothing, but the Incubus's shadows and decibels.

A special thanks to the people who read in my work shop and gave me feed back to this book while I continued to revise for the last ten years.

Linda and Miles Narveson
Dan Aluni of Mystic Suns
Erica Fuss
Marty and Mary Fagnan
Cathy Paguin